A
STRANGER'S
WHISPER

and other dark stories

By

ALAN D. HENSON

© Copyright 2017

The stories presented here are works of fiction. Names, characters, places and incidents are either the product of the author's imagination or are used fictitiously. Any resemblance to actual persons, living or dead, locales, business establishments or events is entirely coincidental.

For information, contact:

E.S.P.
315 E. 53rd St.
Anderson, IN 46013
Email: tazer1229@gmail.com

Printed in the UNITED STATES OF AMERICA

Dedicated to the librarians; keepers of knowledge, wisdom and the archives of time and space. Thank you.

CONTENTS

Fury in the Mind's Eye

It really was a dark and stormy night. The abnormally crooked trees in the cemetery cast wicked shadows across the tombstones. Grave markers were illuminated with each lightning flash. The rumbles of thunder which followed expressed the wrath of the spirits at my presence. I couldn't blame them. I was wondering what I was doing there myself. It must have been some form of temporary insanity which possessed me to come to this isolated unholy place. Unfortunately, my sanity didn't return until it was too late.

If I took my eyes off the twisted trees for a moment and looked back, they seemed to have moved a little closer. The falling rain didn't come directly down from the sky, but crossed the graveyard in a diagonal direction which was more horizontal than vertical. It was more of a spray than a shower and it was disgusting. As it washed over my face, it felt more like saliva or the sweat from an overweight assailant in the night. I tried to wipe it from my mouth and eyes, but the water was quickly replaced by a fresh spray.

I brought a camera, but I left it in the car when the rain started. I wasn't lucky enough to have one of the waterproof kind and I didn't want to ruin it. It was really too bad because some of the images would have been fantastic...eerie, sinister and disturbing, but fantastic. Taking pictures through the windshield would have only produced images of water droplets and blurry images. Besides, staying in the car felt worse than being outside. I know it sounds weird, but there always seemed to be a level of vulnerability inside the car. That was the way it seemed in the horror movies anyway.

Actually, no place here really appeared to be safe. Coming out on a night like this had been a terrible mistake. Even if I left, I wouldn't be able to feel secure...not for a long time. Maybe never again. The images, the sounds and the feelings of dread were burning themselves deep into my brain.

The wind picked up drastically as a heavier part of the storm moved in. The gusts whipped my car antenna and made a whistling/buzzing sound which was reminiscent of the flying saucers in old sci-fi B movies. The woods behind the cemetery came alive with the stronger rush of wind. The trees seemed to be battling to the death and the fiercely rustling leaves were cheering them on. My mind joined in and I began to imagine something enormous coming out of the woods. I heard limbs crack and the leaves began to whip around in a frenzy. It kept coming closer and closer, but I couldn't see it. I was losing my grip on what sanity I had.

There was a noise behind me. I reluctantly took my eyes off the woods to turn and investigate. The large twisted tree seemed much closer than I remembered. Its gnarled limbs resembled skeletal hands which seemed to be reaching for me. Another rumble of thunder caused the ground to shake. An ancient grave marker fell over and my spine froze solid. My legs refused to move, as though they had become rooted to the ground. All I could do was twist at the waist and even that only allowed me to keep an eye on the woods with my limited peripheral vision.

Between the rain and only seeing out of the corner of my eye, my vision was severely compromised, but I was sure I saw something coming out of the woods. The wind was coming in heavy gusts, making it sound as though giant footsteps were approaching. With my frayed nerves, I wasn't sure that they weren't.

Lightning struck an iron post near the road and veins of electricity rippled in all directions from its base. The post seemed to glow long after the lightning strike. It was followed by an immediate crack of thunder which should have caused the earth to open up. My teeth began to chatter from fear and from the cold rain soaking my clothes. Black dots appeared at the corner of my eyes and I was sure I was going to pass out. I couldn't let that happen.

I mustered every ounce of strength I had and forced my left leg to step back. As I did, I felt an intense twinge of pain in my lower back. The tension of an old back injury had been too much. My knees buckled and I fell back. Fortunately, my car was right there and I reached for the handle to support myself. I was able to open the door and practically fell into the driver's seat. Tears formed in the corners of my eyes as I swung my legs inside. I pulled the door shut and held my breath until the pain subsided.

I reached for my keys in the ignition and my heart froze. They weren't there. Had I been stupid enough to take my keys out? What did I do with them? I was so cold and numb, I couldn't tell if they were in my pocket or not. My pants were so wet, they clung to my skin. The denim was abrasive and unyielding as I forced my hand into my front right pocket. I kept digging but I was sure I had left them outside. It felt like Christmas when I finally found them.

My hands were shaking badly and it took me a while to finally get the key into the ignition. I turned the key. Nothing. I tensed up and a back spasm shot down the back of my legs like the lightning strikes I had been witness to. I tried it again…again, nothing. "This didn't happen in real life, did it? A dead car is just a convenient trope for horror movies, right?" I had started to talk to myself, but the voice didn't sound like mine. I held my breath and tried for a third time. The car started right up. I allowed myself to breathe and mumbled something about having to have that looked at. I turned on the windshield wipers and the headlights. Looking back at me through the windshield was the twisted tree.

Between the branches of the tree, eyes like two white-hot embers stared into my soul. The eyes blinked. With each blink, they appeared larger. I was beginning to panic, so I reined in my imagination in an act of self-preservation.

The demonic eyes were the headlights of a vehicle navigating the potholes in the long gravel drive to the cemetery. The vehicle they belonged to was moving incredibly slowly for good reason. Visibility was poor and the potholes were treacherous. The lights disappeared when the vehicle dropped below a rise and then reappeared when it reached a peak. Finally, the vehicle rounded a curve and the lights were completely visible. I began to shake violently and wondered why I had not had the foresight to bring a weapon of any kind. I looked around the dark interior of my car for something...anything. I comically grabbed an ice scraper with a college logo on it. It was small, blue and had a ridiculous cartoon logo on the handle. I don't even remember where I got it. Holding the scraper in my hand gave me a false sense of security, but better than no security at all.

The headlights rounded the top of the cemetery's hill and pointed straight at me. They were joined by a third intense light. When the red and blue lights began flashing, I was relieved but flushed with embarrassment. The spotlight was blinding and nearly obscured the red and blue lights which were defused by the rain and my wipers. Another patrol car had slipped up behind me unnoticed and turned on his lights as well.

A silhouette crossed in front of the blinding lights and made its way to my driver's side door. The officer tapped on my window and I obediently rolled it down. I didn't care if I was going to jail. They could not put me in a holding cell with anyone who would scare me as much as my own imagination had.

"Sir, have you been drinking?" asked the officer. I was surprised to hear a woman's voice. I am not sexist; she just caught me off guard. I actually felt a little more at ease. Maybe I am just a bit sexist. I tried to say that I wasn't drunk, but my teeth were chattering too much for me to be very coherent. The officer seemed to understand and asked for my license and registration.

"I would ask you what you are doing out here at this time of night…in this weather," she said. "…but I really doubt if I could understand you right now."

I forced a smile (which I am sure made me look crazy) and nodded. There had been two officers in each patrol car and the ones who were not checking my registration were shining flashlights around the grounds and into the woods. They were shouting to each other as they did, but I couldn't hear what they were saying because of the wind. It was showing no signs of slowing down even though the rain had stopped for the moment.

Finally, all four of the officers convened at the patrol car behind me. They talked for a few moments before the first officer returned to my window.

"I am afraid we are going to have to take you in," she stated in an almost apologetic way. "We have a few questions for you and you don't appear to be able to answer them right now."

Again, I really didn't mind. Anywhere was better than here. They led me to the first patrol car and eased me into the back. The Plexiglas shield and the lack of door handles made me a little uncomfortable, but the car was toasty warm and I began to thaw. We were halfway to the station before my teeth stopped chattering and at one point it had been so uncontrollable, I thought I might chip my front tooth.

We arrived at the station and I was taken to a squad room instead of being booked. I sat in a comfortable wooden chair next to a desk and the officer (Officer Erica Carmichael) began taking my statement and asked me some questions. I was now much more capable of answering and I tried to be as open and sincere as possible. Plus, I was flirting a little. I blame the element of fear. I also blame the fact that she was gorgeous. Her auburn hair was pulled back into a tight bun, held in place by a black scrunchy. Her long neck was the color of ivory and her deep brown eyes were beautiful, but disarming. I was afraid I would confess to anything if she asked me to.

"Okay," she began. "Really now…what were you doing out there?"

"It seems stupid now, but I went there to get inspired for a book," I responded.

"A book? You went to a creepy old graveyard at night, in a thunderstorm to get inspired to write a book?" I think she was trying to suppress a laugh or anger. She was hard to read.

"Yes, really," I explained. "There are so many horror movies, horror stories, ghost stories, paranormal stories out there; everything has been done. I needed inspiration to try to come up with something fresh. It seemed like a good idea at the time. Now, not so much."

Officer Carmichael inserted a memory card into a slot in her computer and examined the photos from the scene at the cemetery.

"Have you written many novels?" she asked.

"A few," I answered. "Self-published." I tried not to sound apologetic, but I failed.

"So what about the vandalism?" Her tone suddenly turned serious.

"I didn't see any signs of vandalism," I answered. "Nothing recent anyway. There was a marker that fell over when lightning struck, but I didn't do that."

"I mean the serious vandalism that you did," she said. "What was the point of that?"

"What do you mean? I didn't do any vandalism."

"That's not what it looks like," she replied. She was almost fuming now. "We took pictures." Officer Carmichael brought up a series of thumbnail pictures on her screen and began to flip through them one by one.

"Here is where you must have been digging a pit in the ground. Here is another one, and another. Thirteen in all. One was even dug in the ground over a grave. The grave marker was knocked over and broken in half. All the large pits lead back to the woods where you, for some reason, broke several limbs off the trees. Do you want to know what I think?" She didn't wait for an answer. "I think you were trying to create a hoax. Look at this picture!"

The picture she brought up was taken behind the patrol car. The indentations in the ground looked like giant footprints; giant clawed footprints. They led back to a place in the woods where several huge limbs seemed to have been snapped off near their trunks. One of the footprints appeared to have broken the grave marker as if it had been stepped on. I clinched my jaw to keep my teeth from chattering. I had not done any of the damage she was showing me, but it had to be the most elaborate hoax I had ever seen.

"I didn't do any of this damage," I protested. My lower lip trembled like that of a three-year-old. "How could I have done all those things? What would I have used? Search my car! All you're going to find is an ice scraper…and a couple of empty fast food containers. Nothing in my car is capable of doing that kind of destruction."

"We'll see about that," she responded sharply. She grabbed the mic on her collar and radioed the other patrol car.

"Nelson, are you still on the scene?" she asked. The radio crackled and the transmission broke up a lot. "We're still here Erica…sorry, Officer Carmichael. The wind…*crackle* …picking…can't see much…*crackle*…waiting for the tow truck…*snap*."

"Can you search the car and see if you can find any kind of tool or something that could have been used to do all the damage out there?" Officer Carmichael waited for a response. She was about to repeat her request when the radio sparked to life. "Sorry...you broke up...you want us...*crackle*...search for...*crackle*...are you crazy? The wind...so strong, we can't...*buzz*...starting to hail..." There was a sudden thunderclap and the lights in the station went out, as well as all of the lights in town. The police station's emergency generators kicked in, but not quick enough to keep Officer Carmichael from losing all her unsaved data on her computer. She tried to contact Officer Nelson again, but there was nothing but silence on the other end, even when she adjusted the squelch.

The emergency lighting consisted of two sets of flood lamps mounted at each end of the station which cast harsh shadows and did very little to illuminate the room. Thunder continued to roll and lightning flashed through the high grated windows of the building. Officer Carmichael was visibly unnerved by all that was happening. The late shift at the station was only staffed by two deputies and a dispatcher. For some reason, they were all nowhere to be found.

Officer Carmichael hated being left in the dark. She was also in charge, it seemed. She made her first command decision to lock me in a holding cell with the police station's only semi-permanent resident. His name was Castor, but he went by the name of Wolf. He was the town's chief drug-user and was often found passed out in the park near the playground equipment. The cops in town usually tried to make sure he was out of the park by the time any kids showed up. It wasn't that they were worried about him setting a bad example. That ship had sailed a long time ago. They were more worried about what the kids would do to him. They had a habit of drawing on his face with a permanent marker. The station kept a supply of nail polish remover on hand for those occasions. First though, several of the officers would take *selfies* with him.

"I can't just stay around here and do nothing," Officer Carmichael commented. "I will be back in a while and we will sort all this out then."

"I really didn't do anything," I stated. "Do I really have to stay in here? It's not like I'm a murderer or a drug, uh…or a murderer." I looked over at Castor afraid that he was going to take what I said personally. He didn't seem to take offense. He also didn't seem to be conscious.

"You'll be fine," she said. "I shouldn't be that long." I could have continued debating, but she left so abruptly that I almost didn't notice. Thunder rumbled in a way that seemed more ominous than before.

"She's cute," said Castor. Either he was awake the whole time or the thunder woke him. "…but she has a lot of demons if you ask me." I didn't ask, but

I thought it best not to antagonize the man I was locked in a cell with.

"I know you," he said sitting up. "I seen your picture on the back of a book in the library. You're famous."

"I'm self-published," I responded. "I want to be famous."

"You'll get there," he said. "I have faith in you."

"Thanks."

"What are you writing about now?" Castor was having trouble keeping his head level but seemed to be enjoying the sensation.

"I was getting inspiration for a book by spending the night in a cemetery," I answered.

"The haunted cemetery?" He perked up. "The one near the haunted bridge? Or is that the haunted farmhouse near the haunted woods? Did you hear a baby cry?" Castor apparently knew all the local stories and probably had trouble keeping them all straight. "Can I read it?"

"I haven't written it yet," I explained. "…but when I do, I will make sure you get a copy."

"Awesome," said Castor. Then his eyes closed and he fell over hard on the metal bench.

The area around the holding cell was dark. Lightning flashed through the narrow window near the ceiling creating momentary trapezoidal designs on the wall. I couldn't tell if Castor was snoring or clearing his throat, but some kind of sound was coming out of his mouth.

"It's all connected," he softly rasped.

"What's all connected?" I whispered. I wasn't sure he was even talking to me.

"Everything that's happening tonight. Once in a while, things come together just right. There's no reason for it. None that we can see anyway. They just happen; and when they do, watch out!"

"So what happening tonight?"

"Energy, man. Energy mixed with energy." Castor's eyes opened just a bit. "You can't let that much energy meet and not have nothin' happen."

"I still am not sure I know what you are talking about," I responded.

"The storm, dude..." He smiled. "That's one kind of energy. Sounds like a lot of it tonight." I had to admit I was intrigued. "The storm is natural energy," he continued. "That's because it is from Nature."

"Yeah, I get that," I said. I felt like I was being treated like a preschooler.

"The cemetery produces its own energy," he explained. "Its energy is supernatural. Normally we don't notice because we aren't around when it does it. We probably couldn't see it anyway."

"So, don't these two types of energy come together pretty often?" I asked. "I mean, it storms a lot and the cemetery is always there."

"They come together," he answered. "...but tonight was different. There was a third kind of energy out there."

"What kind of energy is that?"

"*Your* kind of energy," he explained. "You were there for inspiration. You opened your unconscious mind to take in all you saw and felt. You opened a door to your darkest nightmares and something came out. The natural energy and the supernatural energy gave it substance; they fed it. Now it sounds like the storm is feeding off of it. It might never stop."

I thought he was going to say more, but his words dissolved into soft snoring. The words may have just been those of a gin-soaked vagrant, but Castor had given me a lot to think about. He definitely gave me something to write about. I watched the patterns of light change shape on the walls and ceiling as the storm continued to rage. I kept listening down the hall for Officer

Carmichael's…Erica's return. Castor was right; she was cute. I was worried about her now.

I leaned into the corner of where the bars of the cell attached to the concrete wall. I must have drifted off myself because when I opened my eyes, I saw that it was morning through the window. It wasn't a bright sunny morning. It was a murky gray daylight; as if the day had stayed out all night drinking and had to go to work the next day. That kind of daylight.

Erica hadn't come back. Neither had any of the other officers as far as I could tell. It wasn't until about 9:30 that someone finally did show up and it wasn't an officer. It was the town's mayor. He was investigating why no one was answering the phone. He almost looked relieved to find someone in the holding cell who could carry on an intelligent conversation with him. He knew better than to ask Castor what was going on.

"What can you tell me?" he asked. "Where is everyone?"

"To tell you the truth, I am not sure. Officer Carmichael left during the storm. As far as I can tell from in here, she hasn't returned from the cemetery."

"Cemetery? Has somebody been fooling around that place again? I thought we were done with all that nonsense when the high school kids went off to college."

"It was just me, I'm afraid," I answered sheepishly. "I was out there when I wasn't supposed to be. They think I vandalized some things."

"Did you?" he asked.

"No, your honor…but I guess there was some damage done."

"Okay," he said with a huff that was probably disgust. "Let's get you out of there. We don't lock people up for vandalism on their first offense. This is your first offense, right?"

"Yes sir…uh, no sir…sorry. I didn't vandalize anything." I just knew he was going to keep me locked up now. Instead, he left and came back with the cell door key. He was smiling in a satisfied way.

"Don't worry son," he said. "I am also the town judge. I know how to make people in the witness box sweat. Now let's see about getting you out of here."

"Do you know if they ever got my car towed in?" I asked. I was afraid to ask for anything more than freedom, but I needed to know.

"I doubt much of anything has been done," he replied. "That storm last night was worse than any I have ever seen; and I have seen a lot of them. I'll take you to your car. It will give me a chance to see what has been going on and to find those officers.

They may be all cozied up in a cruiser getting drunk for all I know. I would be."

Main Street looked like the apocalypse. Huge branches had fallen across the road along with an array of trash cans, bicycles, a couple of kiddie pools and at least one awning. A path had been plowed through the debris; probably by the garbage truck which was not going to try to pick it all up. The mayor headed out of town and tried to reach someone on his own police radio. There was no response. He approached the haunted bridge that Castor spoke of. It was made of iron and painted bone white. It stood out against the gray landscape and hummed as we drove across it. No wonder people thought it was haunted.

Just ahead was the entrance to the cemetery. The iron post that lightning had struck the night before looked melted at the top. The mayor turned into the long drive and I cautioned him about the treacherous potholes. He didn't heed my warning and his car bottomed out...three separate times.

I couldn't see my car from the drive, or much of anything else. A dense fog had rolled in from an adjacent field and rested low to the ground. All that was visible from the drive was the old gnarled tree which was still standing in defiance of the storm. It looked like a black skeletal hand reaching up to the sky, mimicking the lightning forks from the previous night. The drive dipped down to its lowest point and the car sunk below the surface of the fog. Instincts guided the mayor as he rounded the back the drive of the cemetery and we immerged from the mist. His quick reflexes kept us from plowing into the patrol car in the path.

It was facing us and our headlights had almost touched. I had to force myself to see what I was seeing. The patrol car was resting on its roof as if it were a toy and a child had placed it that way. The mayor and I got out of his car to investigate. Other than the weird orientation, nothing else seemed amiss with the cruiser. The keys were even still in the ignition. No one was inside or nearby as far as we could tell.

A shaft of sunlight pierced the gray cloud cover and seemed to evaporate the fog. Walking a few feet, my car came into view. It seemed to be untouched by the storm. However, the battery was dead. Something had caused the engine to die and the keys were left in the ON position. The fog became less like cotton and more like a film…which revealed the other police cruiser. It had not been as fortunate as the other one. It was right-side-up; at least what part of it wasn't twisted in a peculiar angle. Only one of the back wheels could touch the ground. The other stood out parallel to the ground, making the vehicle look like a dog marking its territory. Three horrific claw-like gashes were in the hood and all of the windows were shattered. On the front seat was a clip mic of a police radio...and a black scrunchy. This was Erica's patrol car.

I began to hyperventilate. Black dots once more appeared in my peripheral vision. I felt weak and steadied myself on the hood of the cruiser. I brushed my hand across the rim of one of the gashes in the hood and slashed my palm. A trickle of blood stained the hood and ran down the fender. I felt as if I had probably just contaminated a crime scene.

The fog lifted as rapidly as it had rolled in, giving us an opportunity to survey the damage. I was afraid of what I was going to see. I searched my field of vision for signs of life...or bodies. I didn't see either, but I was probably in denial anyway. The mayor didn't see anything either. What we did see was a cemetery which looked like it was being dug up to make way for a housing development. Almost all of the stones that could be turned over were. Those that were flat markers were half covered with soil. Giant divots in the ground were half-filled with rain water; twenty or so small trees and shrubs were scattered throughout the area.

The trees in the woods behind the cemetery looked as though they had been parted the way a person parts their hair. About halfway in, the part stopped. I stood for a long time at the edge of the woods, but could not force myself to venture in. I suspected that Erica...Officer Carmichael was in there, but I personally would never know.

The mayor finally got in touch with the city impound and they sent a tow truck for my car. They got an outside service to transport the two cruisers. Those cars would be part of an ongoing investigation for some time. No one ever heard from any of the officers again, but I suspect no one had the nerve to search the woods very well.

A couple of weeks passed and I went to the police station to check on the investigation. There wasn't much information they could share. "Things like this just happen," was their official statement. I asked if Castor was being held and if I could go talk to him. It's a small town and they liked Castor in spite of themselves. "You can bail him out if you want," said Officer Sharp. "I think it's still fifty bucks." I suspected the money would go into Officer Sharp's *personal pension fund*, but I didn't care.

I took Castor to the Four-Way-Stop Diner so he could have something besides jail food for a change. He seemed to appreciate it. After a hearty breakfast and into a second carafe of coffee, he seemed more normal and less like a vagrant.

"Do you remember much about the night we shared the holding cell?" I asked.

"Hey man, if I did any of the touchy stuff, I am sorry. I was wacked out of my gourd." Castor looked like he was fashioning an imaginary snowball.

"No," I responded. "Nothing like that. You were very well-behaved. I just wanted to talk to you about a few things you mentioned."

"You're talking about the energies," he said. "I thought I had dreamed that. Funny. I don't remember much about that night, but the dreams seemed as clear as crystal."

"You told me that my imagination opened up a door in my subconscious. That has me worried."

"I suspect so," said Castor. "That's heavy stuff. Some dudes I hang out with sometimes have discussed theories about the energies. We have discussed them with and without being in altered states and our conclusions have always been the same."

"What are your theories?" I asked.

"Are you sure you're ready?" he questioned. "Some of this is not going to be easy to take; and you can't not know it once you know it."

"All I know is that not knowing is killing me," I said.

"Alright. I will try to soften it as much as possible," replied Castor. He took a deep breath and a large gulp of coffee before beginning.

Castor repeated much of what he had told me that night. The energy expelled by the lightning joined with some supernatural energy which was probably always present in the cemetery. There were lots of storms there before. Nothing significant or eerie had ever happened to speak of. The one variable was me. I was there with an open mind. I was taking it all in with the hopes of creating a unique storyline. The elements, both natural and supernatural, combined with the imagination within my unconscious mind and created something so powerful and so horrible that I couldn't control it. In the light of day, I wouldn't let myself search the dark recesses of my being to discover what it might have been.

I would like to think that what occurred was a natural event; a violent display of nature's fury. It would help me sleep at night if it was. I want to believe that those officers who have disappeared will return soon; especially Erica. I would like to see her again and have a chance to get to know her.

The news will report the events that night as yet another tornado in the Midwest. They will mark it in their books as the worst on record. I am racked with guilt. In all probability, my unconscious mind killed Erica Carmichael and the other officers. It may not be true, but I will never convince myself of that. A court wouldn't convict me but I will have already convicted myself. I will have to keep that energy -- that monster that lives within me -- imprisoned. I will have to keep him repressed. We will serve out our life sentence together…in the deepest abyss of my unconscious.

-END-

Extraction

The sense of euphoria was like nothing young Willy had ever experienced. He floated in a womb of darkness like a fully formed embryo. All of his senses were devoid of input except for touch; and even that consisted of nothing but a general feeling of ambient temperature. He was warm. Perhaps warmer than should have been comfortable, but he didn't care. He became aware of the sensation of floating and embraced it spiritually. He thought that this must be what heaven feels like.

Willy began to become aware of more things. He suddenly knew where he was. He was in his bedroom. He was floating three feet above his bed and did not seem to feel that that was unusual. On the other side of the room, Willy's brother Russell snored quietly in the darkness. If he only knew…he thought. Willy wanted the feeling to go on forever. He was sure that it must be what getting high feels like; even though he had never been high.

Willy was eleven and pretty inexperienced in such things. The more he involved himself in the feeling, the more aware he became. Gravity began to tug at him; increasing ever so slightly with the passing seconds. The ticking of the clock that at seemed so silent, was increasing in volume. He felt his mattress beneath him as his own weight pressed him snuggly into his sheets. He tried to hold on to his euphoria, but the heat of the room had become stifling. Sweat trickled from his forehead and into his ears, causing him to shiver. He tried to remain relaxed; but it was as if his body had other plans.

Willy didn't know how he knew, but something was about to happen. It wasn't anything he hadn't experienced before, but in this case he had done nothing to initiate it. He felt another warm trickle above his upper lip and this time he knew it wasn't sweat. Blood gushed forth from his nose in a steady stream and Willy bolted upright in a panic. Perspiration ran down into his eyes and he couldn't see as he hurried to the bathroom. Blinded and bleeding, he hit the wall in the hallway staining it with blood spatters and finger streaks. He fumbled his way to the bathroom and turned the cold water on full.

Willy splashed water on his face and searched for a clean washcloth to soak in cold water. He held his head back as he had been taught and pressed the cold compress under his nose. Gagging a little as he felt blood trickle down his throat he stood in the middle of the bathroom with his head back, waiting. He thought it was a little comical because he was waiting for the bleeding to stop the way one waits at the corner for the crosstown bus. Then he became impatient. The bleeding was taking longer to stop than he thought it ought to.

Willy's mother came down the hall to investigate the noise. She investigated every noise in the night. She stifled a gasp when she saw the bloodstains on the hallway wall and carpet. Her gasp became audible when she saw the bathroom. It all looked like a crime scene. All that was missing was the yellow police tape and evidence markers. She made sure that Willy was not injured and consoled him the best she could. Then she started cleaning up the blood on the tile with a wet towel. Since he was okay, she gave him disapproving looks each time she wrung out the towel into the toilet.

Willy's bleeding didn't look like it was going to stop and he was seriously concerned that he might have to go to the hospital. His dad finally came to investigate and was not nearly as concerned with Willy's wellbeing. Instead, he was more concerned as to how they were going to get the blood out of the carpet; as if putting it there had been intentional. He would have liked to have gone back to bed since he had to get up for work in a few hours; but there would be no point if he was going to have to drive Willy to the hospital. He had just gone back to his room to get dressed when Willy's mom called to him and said that the bleeding had finally stopped.

Willy's nose had bled a full fifty minutes. His parents should have already taken him to the hospital, but he lucked out and didn't die it seemed. His father grumbled about the trouble he caused and went back to bed. His mother kissed him on the head and reassured him that everything was alright. Willy went back to bed and tried in vain to recapture his euphoria. The night was terribly hot and the air just hung in the room like a thick blanket. There was no hint of a breeze blowing through the window and the night was deadly silent. Not even the cicadas were making noise.

Willy's sheets were soaked with sweat. He hadn't noticed how soaked before because he had been preoccupied. Now they were cold in spite of the heat and they gave him a chill. The chill didn't last long and he tried to go to sleep. He began wondering what had caused his nosebleed and what had led up to it. His mind was buzzing with theories, so going to sleep seemed to be out of the question. He thought back to things he had read that fit his circumstances.

The first thing that came to mind was something he remembered reading. There were also television shows about similar events and even a couple of movies. The programs were about people who had been abducted by aliens and didn't remember it happening. Under hypnosis, they had recalled how they felt as if they were being levitated out of their beds and felt very euphoric. Some had reported unusual nosebleeds and small metallic objects showed up in their x-rays. They also said the weather during those abductions had been unseasonably warm. Willy touched his nose and wondered. It made him feel kind of special and afraid at the same time. He remembered dreaming about an alien craft, but it was located in a place that would have been way too public to go unnoticed. Willy was pretty sure that was just a dream. Besides, he remembered countless alien creatures running into the craft which could not possibly had contained them all.

Had Willy drifted off to sleep at that point, he would probably have dreamed of aliens again. He didn't, however; and he continued to explore other possibilities. One theory came from a book he had read recently. It wasn't science fiction in the conventional sense. It was more like a self-help book about one's own spiritual being. Someone had left the book behind at the bus stop or Willy wouldn't have even found it. Something in the first few pages intrigued him. It seemed to contradict formal religions and yet agree with them on several points. He read about how the human soul was composed entirely of light, yet was attached to the physical body by a single silver thread. It said that should that thread ever break, the soul would be freed from the body and the physical body would die. He wondered if that was what happened to people in comas; if their silver threads snapped and their souls left their bodies behind.

Willy considered the possibility that his soul had tried to leave his body. He wondered if he had been fighting for his own soul and if that was why he was bleeding. It didn't make sense to him in some ways. In other ways it did. He had read about astral projection and how people could go all over the world and still be connected to their bodies by the thread. As far as he could tell, his soul only got three feet above his bed. If he was experiencing astral projection, his physical body was keeping him on a pretty short leash.

Those thoughts led Willy to darker possibilities. What if something was trying to steal his soul and he was fighting back? He didn't know how to process that thought and tried to turn from it. In his mind, he tried to go to a pleasant place; a place where nothing bad ever happened. In his safe place, there was a willow tree and its long whip-like tendrils dipped into the crystal surface of a pond. Willy lay on his side and relaxed in the shade of the tree on a mild summer afternoon. The sunlight winked at him through the leaves as a soft breeze blew. A nap would have been just the thing, but Willy wanted to fully experience his fantasy.

The soft breeze picked up and the willow tree began to whip the surface of the pond like an unruly child. Willy had been punished that way and he didn't like it. The sky darkened with threatening clouds. Willy tried to move but was paralyzed in his now fetal position on the bank of the pond. A soft spray drenched his face and threatening clouds dipped lower. Wisps of dark mist moved closer to the surface of the water. The mist took shape in a way Willy had never seen. He could make out a cluster of beings, but their images were vague. All he could tell was that they were as threatening as the approaching storm.

Willy thought he heard thunder in the distance with voices concealed in the rumble. He was terrified but still could not move. He gave them a name. *Soul Stealers*, he thought. They were there to take his soul; he was certain of that. He was sure his nose had begun to bleed again as he braced himself against their attack. He squinted his eyes as tightly as he could and waited for the inevitable grip of their icy fingers. Darkness closed in around him completely and he was sure that his life was over. He was too tired to go on and at last, gave in. A feeling of peace washed over him.

Then Willy heard birds chirping. A gentle breeze waft across his face and he could hear the soft chatter of maple leaves outside his window. He had fallen asleep after all. The heatwave of the night had given way to a most pleasant summer day. Willy wasn't sure he was really awake and cautiously peeked out through his closed eyelids. The room was softly lit by morning sunlight and was cool enough that he needed his sheet to keep the chill away. He breathed a sigh of relief like he had never know. He had kept the soul stealers away, even though he was sure they were part of his vivid imagination. He smiled and planned to go back to sleep when his mother came in and ruined that idea.

"Get up you two," she said. "I've got a lot of cleaning to do today after last night and you are going to help."

"Sorry mom," said Willy. He sheepishly got out of bed and headed for the hall.

"You can have breakfast first," she said. "I'm not a tyrant." Willy smiled and went to the kitchen. He could hear his mother's exasperated tone as she tried to wake his brother. Russell was either a very solid sleeper or a very good faker. His mother was getting angry. Willy knew that because she was using his middle name.

"Russell Michael..." she yelled! "Russell? Russell? Wake up!" His mother's tone had turned alarming. Willy ran back to his bedroom. His mother was shaking Russell by the shoulders trying to wake him. Willy stood at the end of his brother's bed and stared at him. Two trails of dried blood led from Russell's nostrils and two pools of blood had stained his sheets. His eyes were not quite closed and Willy was pretty sure Russell wasn't breathing. Willy began to cry.

-END-

The Bell Curve

A midlife crisis can take on many forms. Some guys get a sports car or a motorcycle. Others have affairs. Some do all or none of those things. They are all vain attempts to recapture the past or a misspent youth.

Rodney Morelle was no different. He wasn't thrilled about turning fifty and it sneaked up on him years before he thought it should. He was half a century old and felt like he had been cheated out of the entire first half of his life. The job he had was not the job he had sought when he graduated from high school. It was a tedious job and paid just well enough to keep him with the company. He was never going to get rich, but the company had a decent retirement plan and the insurance benefits were not too shabby.

But Rodney always felt he was destined for greater things. He felt that he had missed out in high school because of his low self-esteem. If he could have gone back and talked to his younger self, he would have told him to be more serious about school, work harder, take chances and make the most of his youth. It didn't matter. His younger self wouldn't have listened to him anyway. The young always think they are immortal. They think getting older only comes with perks like getting drunk and having sex anytime they want it. He was so naïve back then.

Rodney looked at the large sheet cake his co-workers got him for his fiftieth birthday. It was decorated with white frosting with black trim. In the center was a black skull and crossed bones. "It was either this or the Grim Reaper," said Stan. Stan was usually in charge of department celebrations because his sister owned a bakery.

"Those were the only two options?" he asked. He faked a smile, but he was dead serious.

"There was a tombstone design," said Stan. "...but I thought that would be too morbid."

"Well," said Rodney. "It's the thought that counts." A few of his co-workers caught his sarcasm. Most just ignored it and suggested that he cut the cake. He took a plastic knife and prepared to seriously butcher the cake when Marjorie spoke up.

"Not like that! Let me do it." She took the knife from his hands and pulled out a box of dental floss. Using a length of floss, she cut out of grid of cake portions with laser-like precision. Marjorie worked in the engineering department.

Rodney felt the weight of his mortality crushing him. Other than the cake, there was not much more to Rodney's celebration. There were no balloons, no presents; nothing. It was like any other day at work. After work, there was no surprise party waiting for him. He lived alone and his kids lived a thousand miles away. There were voicemails from them and he got a few birthday cards from people who remembered that it was his birthday; but no celebration. He treated himself to a steak at one of the better restaurants in town, but he didn't tell anyone it was his birthday. If they made a big deal about it, he would just look sad and desperate.

He sulked as he ate his steak. It was prepared just the way he liked it, rare but no blood; but it might as well have been a cheap chopped steak cut. His mind had been so preoccupied, he hadn't enjoyed eating it. Rodney hardly realized he had been eating it at all until it was almost gone. By then it was too late and another birthday was shot to hell. Rodney did order a second glass of merlot. *At least I can enjoy this*, he thought. He didn't though. His thoughts had turned to thinking about how life should have been by this time in his life. A half century had passed since he entered the world. He thought he should have more to show for it. Upon entering college, his goal had been to get into advertising. He had expected to be a chief executive by the time he was forty. Forty came and went and he was still at the same job. Rodney had never finished college, so his dreams were put on hold forever. He could have gone back to college, but in his mind, his life was more than half over, so he didn't see the point. In twelve years, he could draw his pension. Three more years or so after that, he would be on Social Security and Medicare. He felt like he was aging faster just thinking about it. Twelve years had seemed like such a long time when he was twenty. Now it seemed like it was only a few weeks away.

Rodney had one more glass of wine and took a cab home. He got into his comfy clothes and logged on to his social network accounts to respond to his birthday well-wishers. There were more than he expected even though he knew a lot of them only remembered because of reminders on their pages. Still, it was the thought that counted. He checked his email account and was surprised to see the name of Daphne Houten, a friend from high school. He almost missed it because the subject line looked like spam. It said: I'VE HAD A BREAKTHROUGH. WE NEED TO TALK!

Daphne Houten was Doctor Daphne Houten now and had been Rodney's friend in high school; one of only a few. Initially, he hadn't struck up a conversation with her because she was very pretty, very smart and clearly out of his league. She was the one who spoke to him first and left him speechless. Girls like Daphne Houten didn't talk to him. Once he got over his initial shock, he developed a crush on her. It was a crush he would never act upon, but never really got over. She was tall, beautiful and much more mature than most of the other girls his age.

Even in eleventh grade, she carried herself like a successful professional. Rodney knew that she would be successful one day.

They sat next to each other in *English Lit* and she was the first to break the ice by noticing his artwork. He had been doodling in the margin of his homework assignment when she remarked as to how talented he was. She also told him that the teacher was likely to take points off for his artistic illustrations. Some teachers were like that back then. Daphne and he were good friends after that. It was like they had always known each other; maybe in a past life.

Daphne encouraged Rodney to improve his grades and buckle down. She helped him with some of the subjects he was a little slow in and he drew cartoon illustrations in the margins of his notebook to make her laugh. Daphne was probably the reason Rodney didn't drop out of school. She really seemed to be proud of him when he succeeded and that made all the difference to him. It would have been easy to fall in love with her, but again, Rodney knew that she was out of his league and that he could never truly make her happy. Her rejection would have ripped his heart in half and he would have died; inside anyway. Instead, he cherished her as a friend and didn't want to spoil that relationship. They kept in touch after graduation as well as they could. Daphne went away to a college in the east, while Rodney struggled with community college at home.

Doctor Daphne Houten was a respected researcher in the field of genetics and bioengineering. Her work was mysterious because only a few could grasp her abstract concepts; and she didn't confide in very many people about it. Her email to Rodney had only consisted of a few cryptic lines and a time and place for a meeting. Rodney was less curious about whatever her breakthrough was and more excited about seeing Daphne in person again. He responded right away and ignored the fact that she had not even mentioned his birthday. She had been the one person on whom he could count on not forgetting.

Daphne wrote that Rodney should meet her in a coffeehouse the next day not too far from his apartment. He was nervous and excited when he arrived at 4:30 on the dot. Daphne was already there, sitting at a small French café table in the corner sipping from a cup with the name DAFNEY misspelled on it. She had a bright red laptop in front of her and was staring intently at the screen. Rodney gasped when he saw her. She literally didn't look a day older than the last time he saw her. If anything, she looked younger. He had last seen her at their ten year class reunion twenty-two years before. Her hair was the same color of copper that he remembered and her translucent skin was like porcelain. He paused for a moment to reflect on her beauty and considered his own appearance with disdain. What hair he had left was no longer dark brown, but salt-and-pepper; heavy on the salt. Daphne didn't seem to have a single wrinkle and her eyes were as blue and as sharp as ever. They crinkled ever so slightly in a mischievous way when she saw him standing there.

Daphne motioned him over which snapped him out of his trance. She stood up and embraced him for a long time. The scent of her perfume filled his nose and he held on to her for longer than he probably should have. He was blushing when he finally released her and was sure he would see rebuke in her eyes. Instead, he was sure he saw gratitude. His blush faded into a warm feeling all over.

"I am so glad you came," she said. "I know this was short notice."

"I would drop everything for you," he said. He realized that sounded a little desperate, so he qualified it with, "...besides, it's not like I have that much going on in my life." That felt like it sounded pathetic. Daphne didn't seem to notice.

"Order your drink," she said. "...and then come sit next to me. I am really excited about this." Rodney did as instructed and sat down to wait for his café mocha to be prepared. He tried to be cool and detached but he felt a bolt of electricity when their thighs touched. He thought Daphne might have felt it too when she looked in his eyes and said, "I have waited so long to share this with someone and you are the only person in the world that I…"

"Rodney," shouted the barista. Rodney's trance was broken and he wished he had used his last name for his order. He felt awkward and a little annoyed as he retrieved his drink and went back to the table. Daphne's excitement no longer seemed sensual and it probably shouldn't have in the first place. Rodney had a bad habit of overestimating his relationships. Daphne was all business now and Rodney had to hide his disappointment.

"This isn't going to mean anything to you, but I have been working on this project for over fifteen years." Daphne turned the laptop toward Rodney and showed him a three-dimensional representation of a chemical compound. Rodney raised one eyebrow and tried to look scholarly, but it didn't make him any smarter. Finally, he gave up trying.

"I have no idea what I am looking at," he said. "It reminds me a little of tinker toys."

"I know," said Daphne. "I wondered how long it would take before you gave in and admitted that." She lowered her voice and leaned in close when she spoke. Her soft breath was an intoxicating mix of spearmint and latte. Keeping his concentration was going to be an uphill battle until she told him what she had discovered.

"It's a rejuvenation compound," she whispered.

"You mean like those face creams that are supposed to make you look younger," he asked?

"Those things are not even in the same ballpark as this," she said. "This compound can make a person younger at a cellular level."

Rodney didn't know what to say. He cared deeply for Daphne and he didn't want to doubt her; but her claim was pretty unbelievable.

"I know it seems fantastic," she said. "There is still a lot of things to work out, but this research is very promising."

"Okay," said Rodney. "Fill me in on the details, but please keep it simple. Have you tried this on anyone yet?"

"I have tried it on lab animals mostly," said Daphne. "The results have been very consistent. The compound has had a side effect of curing diseases that were genetic in some subjects. It's a shame there are so many hoops to jump through to get approval for human trials."

"So you haven't tried it on a human subject then?"

"Only one," she whispered. "...but I wasn't supposed to."

"What were the results there?" he asked.

"You tell me. You're looking at them," she said.

"You tried it on yourself? Have you never seen a horror movie?" Rodney realized his whisper had increased in volume.

"It's safe," said Daphne. She placed her hand on his to hush his tone. "I wouldn't have tried it if I wasn't confident that it would work. I've been administering it for over a year with no ill effects."

"So how do you know it had any effect at all," he asked? "You were always one of those people with good genes."

"Was I? Let me show you something. This is from four years ago." Daphne brought up a series of pictures on her laptop. They showed a woman in her seventies in a hospital gown sitting on an examination table. Her sunken face was framed by a straw-like thresh of gray hair.

"I won't go into what I was diagnosed with," she said. "…but I had less than a year to live."

"This is you?" Rodney stared incredulously at the picture; trying to make his eyes accept what Daphne had just told him. "That's not possible!"

"It's me," she said. "So you see, I had little choice than to take the chance when it came along. I was just hoping for a cure. I that this would be a side effect." She pulled up a picture of herself at the beach in a bikini. Rodney might have been aroused by it had it not been for the picture he had just seen before. It could easily have been from a photoshoot for Sports Illustrated.

"I need a minute," he said. He sat silently and thought back to high school. The girl who had been so friendly and encouraging then was sitting next to him right now. Her story was so fantastic that he was having a hard time wrapping his head around it. Yet the evidence was right there, sipping a latte and looking radiant. Instead of playing devil's advocate, he chose to accept her claims on faith.

"I know you don't believe me," she said. "...and I don't expect you to; not without proof. That is why I am here."

"I don't understand," said Rodney.

"I have a limited authorization to conduct human testing," she said. "One subject only and five years of observation."

"You want me to be the subject? Why me?"

"There are a number of reasons," said Daphne. "We know what the results are on a terminal subject. Now we want to know how it works on someone who is relatively healthy. I thought of you because of your background. Your family is genetically prone to cancer, but you haven't seemed to show any signs of it...yet. Statistically, you probably will soon."

Daphne's tone had suddenly turned very clinical and a bit ominous. Rodney felt the hair standing up on his arms. Daphne noticed his apprehension and softened her tone.

"Besides," she said. "I remember the kid you were in school. You were always sort of a geek. Loveable, but still a geek. I thought if anyone deserved a second chance at youth, it should be you."

A ripple of energy felt like it penetrated Rodney's chest. He was deeply flattered and quite flustered. There was so much to think about and so many emotions to process. His mouth was dry and he took a sip of his mocha before he spoke again.

"So what's involved here?" he asked. His voice broke once and his question had to be restated.

"There will be a series of injections; I am sorry about that." Daphne knew he hated needles. "Other than that, just bombardment with a very low level of radiation."

"Radiation?"

"Nothing to worry about," she said. "It's just to jumpstart the cellular reconstruction. You won't turn into a hulk or anything."

"Do you have a name for your procedure," he asked? "You will need to market it if it is successful."

"That brings us to the only downside of the compound," she said.

"Of course there had to be a downside," said Rodney. "There's always a downside. Okay, what is it?"

"I call the procedure Bell Curve." Daphne stated the title as if she were submitting her dissertation. "I call it that because of how it works and the estimated length of its effect."

"Go on." Rodney tried and failed to appear scholarly again.

"The positive results begin right away, show signs of anti-aging within a few months," she began. "After a year or so, the subject should have the chronological physique and appearance of someone in their thirties. Within ten years, the subject will have progressed...or maybe I should say regressed, to a point of peak physical maturity; namely, their early twenties."

"I am not seeing a downside here," said Rodney. "You said there was a downside." Daphne paused for a long time. She brought up a graph that did indeed have a bell curve.

"From what we have been able to determine from our lab experiments," she said. "...the results are pretty conclusive. Once a subject reaches their optimum physical age, their cells began to slowly break down so that they don't repair themselves as quickly. The subjects still maintain their youth, but there seems to be an unintended programmed expiration date built into the process."

"Expiration date?"

It's not as bad as it sounds," said Daphne. "Our estimates are that human subjects live to well into their seventies; maybe eighty years old before their cells start to break down completely. That is if the subject is in his or her forties when the process is first administered. Test subjects who are younger will probably burn out much earlier."

"So you are telling me that if I submit to this procedure, I will get younger until I am seventy-five or so and then just die?" Rodney wasn't sure how to take what he was hearing.

"It may not be that way for everybody," said Daphne. "This procedure is still very experimental. Many more trials will need to be conducted before we can draw any accurate conclusions. Imagine though, if you were terminally ill."

"But I'm not," said Rodney.

"Aren't you? Aren't we all, really? Look, we all thought we would try to grow old gracefully, but that was because we had to. Now we don't."

Rodney couldn't argue with her logic. He had been presented with a philosophical question at most. Would one rather live the last part of his life with youth and vigor; knowing almost exactly when he is going to die? Or would he rather grow old as nature intended; never knowing when the end would come? When he thought about it that way, it didn't seem like he had that much to lose. Of course, he wasn't in the best frame of mind to begin with. Daphne's proposal seemed like a passive form of suicide. It would just take a very long time to carry it out.

"What if they develop more drugs to extend a person's lifespan," he asked?

"We have the same chance of extending ours," she said. "Even more so, because of our field of research. Come on Rodney; be young with me...again." If Rodney had any reservations, they dissolved with Daphne's sincere request.

"When do we start?" he asked.

* * *

When Rodney was a child, the years crept by like a prison sentence. It felt as though twenty months passed from one Christmas to the next. When he turned twenty-one, time moved a bit faster, but he hardly noticed the speedup. When he hit thirty, he wondered when has life had begun to gain so much momentum. He looked back on his twenties and regretted some of the chances he didn't take and opportunities that he had missed. By the time his forties rolled around, the years were careening down the slope of time like an out of control *Radio Flyer*.

The panel of compounds Rodney received from Daphne did just as they were promised. He felt more rejuvenated the very next week. The transformation was so sudden that it made him nervous. Nothing that felt that good so quickly could possibly be safe. Still, he continued his treatments for as long as Doctor Daphne said that he should. Within a month, his salt and pepper beard had darkened so that he had only a distinguished streak of gray in it. That was gone a month later.

Something that also surprised Rodney was that his hair had begun to come back in. It was a surprising and welcome side-effect. He didn't think it was possible to overcome the baldness gene. He actually had to start using conditioner for the first time in almost thirty years. Rodney had begun to go bald right out of high school. That had not helped his confidence and it would be another five years before his age would grow into his appearance. One the plus side, he never got carded at liquor stores and bars back then. On the negative side, he wasn't much of a drinker.

Rodney's rejuvenation treatments were no longer necessary after four years. He required a checkup every six months, but those were just routine. He went back more often, but that was only because he wanted to see Daphne. His youthful appearance was catching up to hers and she informed him that there would be a lag in the anti-aging process for what she estimated as between two and five years. Since they were the first two human guinea pigs to receive the treatment, she was using data from actual guinea pigs. Rodney didn't mind the lag. His appearance was that of someone in their late twenties or early thirties. He also thought he looked better than he did when he was actually that age. He definitely felt better.

Rodney saw Daphne socially a few times a month and went back to college to complete his degree. His newfound youth gave him greater drive and level of focus. By using credits for *life experience* and several he had obtained online, Rodney had his degree within two years. He got a new job with an ad agency and left his menial job behind; along with his pension plan. He rationalized that he didn't need it since he was going to be young until he died and he didn't want any reminders of his past life.

Daphne ran into an obstacle getting her *rejuvenation formula* approved by the FDA. There were enough side effects in her lab animals that the board felt more testing was warranted. She tried to tell them that human trials had shown no ill effects, but they wouldn't listen. She was trapped in a Catch-22 until she could eliminate side effects in primates.

Daphne and Rodney began to grow apart. She began turning him down when he asked her out. She was stressed by her clinical frustration and threw herself into her work. Rodney thought that she felt that their relationship had run its course. He thought he felt the same way, but somehow he knew deep down that he didn't.

What he had begun feeling was a resurgence of raging teenage hormones. Daphne had told him to expect that effect and that it was normal. Rodney suspected that Daphne's had been raging for some time since she had started the treatments two years before he did. What he didn't know was that she had experienced another spike in hormones while she was in her faux-thirties. It wasn't that she wasn't interested in sex at the same time as Rodney. It was that her work and her relationship seemed at odds with each other making it hard to focus on both. She chose her work.

Rodney on the other hand, felt like his hormones were out of control. All of the women in the ad agency seemed to be aggressively trying to get him into bed. Some of them actually were. He held out for a long time before he finally succumbed to their advances. His hormones were so out of control that he experienced something he had not had to deal with since he was in high school math class. Back then, he had to refuse to work out problems on the board; taking a zero for the day rather than display the outline of his impromptu erection to the class and submit himself to humiliation. Lately, he had to make several of his ad campaign presentations sitting down because of embarrassing surprise visits from his suddenly alert *Johnson*. He knew he needed to fix that particular problem before he ended up losing his job so he solved it buy buying an athletic supporter and pants that were much looser. It wasn't very stylish, but at least it meant fewer visits to Human Resources.

Rodney's hormone issue finally leveled off and he was able to fend off proposed office romances. He had invested much of his money and received a few bonuses. By the time he was sixty-five, he had a pretty good nest egg put back. He filed for Social Security and was able to live comfortably without his company salary. He gave his two-week notice and slipped quietly out of the company workforce without too many people noticing.

Daphne, while as beautiful as ever, was approaching seventy and knew she didn't have many years left. She signed an agreement with her fellow researchers that if ever the treatment was approved, it would be named after her. She also had an agreement in an ironclad contract that her share would go to her heirs; even though she didn't have any. Rodney arrived for his checkup and was surprised by the change in Daphne's demeanor. She seemed at ease for the first time in years. Daphne thought Rodney also looked more at ease. The ad agency must have been more stressful on him than either of them had realized.

She readily accepted his request when he asked her to go out and she did not refuse when he suggested that they go back to his apartment. In fact, she was quite eager. Their night of earth-shaking passion became the first of many. They had the best of both worlds; the stamina of youth and the experience of age. Their inhibitions were a thing of the past and their sex life was creative and satisfying; so satisfying.

Then as quickly as it began, their relationship was over. Daphne simply vanished. One day while Rodney was out, Daphne cleared out every item she had kept at his apartment; even a nearly empty tube of toothpaste for sensitive teeth. Rodney searched desperately for her, but either no one knew where she had gone, or no one was talking. He struggled to determine what he might have done wrong and why she had left him.

There may have been a few signs something was wrong. Daphne had sat quietly sometimes with her eyes welling up and other times he heard her crying in the bathroom. When he asked her about it, she just said it was *female stuff* and he knew better than to question her after that. Still, she didn't seem to harbor any ill feelings about him as far as he could tell. Now she was just gone.

Rodney tried not to blame himself for her departure, but that was impossible. He blamed himself for everything. He hadn't cheated on her while they were a couple. He was a gentleman and didn't talk about former lovers and she had been equally as respectful. He had thought they were happy. His recaptured youth brought with it the heartache that only a teenager truly knows. He cried openly when he was alone, which was most of the time. He lost a lot of weight because, in addition to his increased metabolism, he was an emotional wreck and didn't eat.

Rodney had distanced himself from everyone he knew except Daphne and had no one to talk to. There was no one else he could relate to anyway. He was out of touch with people who were his physical age, but couldn't relate to people his chronological age. He found that youth, like so many other things in life, isn't that great if you have no one to share it with. As the months passed, he felt like a condemned man awaiting his sentence to be carried out. Then, on his seventieth birthday, he got an email from Daphne. Rodney was almost afraid to open it. He gathered up his courage and clicked on the envelope icon next to her name. The email didn't start with a casual birthday greeting as he had expected. Instead, it was very sincere and to the point. Rodney held his breath as he read it.

"Dearest Rodney," she began. *"I never wanted to hurt you, but some things are just beyond our control. Getting old does not always bring wisdom with it. I was so excited about the prospects of my*

experiments that I didn't consider all of the consequences. When two people grow old together, they almost become one person. They settle into a rhythm or a routine that perfectly syncs together. They tend to know what the other is thinking and react in a kind of synchronized ballet. We didn't get that chance. We grew young together and that was completely uncharted territory.

"I knew my time must have been getting close and I didn't want you to see me deteriorate before your eyes. I never wanted to see disappointment on your face. Still, that isn't the reason I left. Initially, I had only intended to leave until I sorted things out. One serious thing followed another and only now do I feel that I must contact you. My conscience won't let me keep silent any longer. Open the attachment within this email before reading the rest."

Rodney clicked on the attachment and looked at the picture Daphne had sent. Daphne's crystal blue eyes peered out from the photo with a level of innocence he had never seen in her. Her curly copper colored hair framed the porcelain features of a very young toddler. He had the sudden realization that this was the side effect that had halted her studies. Her youth must have regressed well back beyond her original expectations. She now had the mind of an adult in the body of a child. He wondered how much farther she would regress before she would stop. He read the rest of her email.

"Just like in chronological youth, accidents happen. I suspect you think that the picture I attached is me. It's not. It is a picture of our daughter Kryssi. She was conceived about two months before I left. I didn't know what to do and I needed time to think. I seriously considered terminating the pregnancy, but I couldn't do it; even though I knew what that meant. I am sorry for not including you in the decision. I was wrong for that. I know that now. Especially since I have to now ask you what I must.

"I am not trying to be clinical here, but she is a continuation of my experiments; even though she was not intended to be such. While I was considering termination, it came to me that she is the product of two people who regained their youth. There is no telling whether she will live past childhood or if she will live to be two hundred years old. As I said, accidents happen. I won't be here to find out, but you possibly could be. The lab continued with my trials and have had some promising results; just not in time to help me it seems. If you agree, I have given them instructions to give you the new experimental panel of treatments and to monitor your progress or lack thereof. The worst that could happen I think, is that you will follow in my path. I don't mean to be morbid, but that was what you signed up for. This may be a loophole in that contract. If it works, your life could be prolonged by another fifty years. That could be enough time for you to see our daughter

grow up. It might also allow enough time for research to permanently conquer this thing we call death. All I ask is you think about it.

"Please don't try to contact me. It is too late for that anyway. Kryssi is staying with my niece in Albany. Her address and number are at the bottom of this email. I am so sorry for the pain you have now and will experience because of me. We really should have dated in school. Too late to worry about that now. I guess youth isn't just wasted on the young. I love you. I always have. Take care, no matter what you decide to do.

"All my love, Daphne."

Rodney sat silently for what seemed like an hour. He kept wondering if he had just dreamed what he read. He read the email again and stared at the picture. Closer examination let him see some of his own traits in the face of the child; subtle as they were. A feeling washed over him he had never felt before, even in his youth. He was a dad now. He had a daughter. It excited him and ironically made him feel young. Despite what Daphne had said, he needed to see her.

Rodney knew Daphne had moved out of her own apartment long ago; so he went to the only place he could, in hopes of catching her there. The researchers at her lab looked as if they had been expecting him. They must have thought he was there to begin the new panel of drugs. They nodded knowingly when he said that for now, he was only trying to find Daphne.

"You should wait in Doctor Farr's office," said one of the researchers that Rodney only knew as Dave. He didn't question him and went obediently to the office. In a few minutes, Doctor Farr came in and uncharacteristically sat in the chair next to Rodney rather than behind his desk. He waited for a moment before he spoke.

"There is no easy way to say this," he said. "...but Daphne died three days ago. Her congenital illness, while in regression, was particularly aggressive once her treatments were no longer effective. I am very sorry. We loved her very much as I feel you must have. We even asked her if we should contact you, but she asked us not to. Her appearance had progressed well beyond her years. In the end, she was physically twice as old as she was chronologically. The price of youth I guess." Rodney was speechless. It was a good thing that he had been given the gift of a second youth because the news would have probably killed him otherwise.

"I don't expect you to decide right away," said Doctor Farr. "...but I wouldn't wait too long to begin the new program. We will need time to run some tests and go over the possible side effects." Then his tone softened. "You should go see your daughter first before deciding. I am sure that is what Daphne would have wanted." Rodney began to cry uncontrollably and Doctor Farr didn't know whether to hug him or let him be alone. In the end, he patted him on the shoulder and gave him the room.

Rodney left the lab with red eyes and a large manila envelope containing Daphne's will, Kryssi's birth certificate and a lengthy handwritten letter that must have been composed over several weeks. He read some of it in his car but stopped when it looked like she had finished a thought. He looked at the birth certificate. Krishna Daphne Morelle had been born on May 6th, two years earlier. Kryssi was named after the Hindu god of rebirth. Rodney thought that was most fitting.

The town of Albany was only three hours away and Daphne's niece welcomed Rodney like she had known him her whole life. Her name was Piper and he liked her immediately. She had Daphne's smile, wit and porcelain features, but her hair and eyes were dark brown. He sat in a soft chair in the living room while Piper prepared some tea. Rodney wasn't much of a tea drinker, but he thought it would be rude to decline. She returned with the tea and sat on the other side of an end table.

"Aunt Daphne told me so many things about you," she said.

"I am sorry," said Rodney. "I didn't even know you existed until today."

"That's alright," said Piper. "She was kind of secretive when it came to family. I guess it was for our protection; though I am not sure why she thought we needed it."

"Me either," said Rodney. There was an awkward pause in the conversation. Then Piper broke the silence.

"I guess there are some things you need to know about your daughter," she said. A chill went down Rodney's spine when she spoke. He was still getting used to being a parent after so many decades of being single. Piper continued.

"I know the whole story about the drugs and stuff," she said. "I must say, you look even younger than I expected."

"I doubt that will last too much longer," said Rodney.

"You never know," said Piper. "Things tend to work out sometimes." Her positive attitude made Rodney smile.

"Kryssi is very special," she said abruptly. "I am not just saying that because she is my cousin. I have never seen a little girl so smart for her age. She is reading at a fourth grade level already. I wasn't even out of diapers at her age."

"I am not sure if that is good or bad," said Rodney. His solemn tone brought the mood down.

"I don't like to think of the bad," said Piper. "Only the good. I think Kryssi is going to lead the way to a whole universe of discoveries."

"I hope you're right," said Rodney. "Would it be okay if I saw her?"

"I thing that would be great," said Piper. "I'll go get her." She left the room and Rodney could hear her softly calling for Kryssi in an impromptu game of hide-n-seek.

"She'll never find me." A smiling porcelain face peered out from under the end table. "I've been here the whole time. She isn't very good at this game."

When Rodney finally found his voice, he said, "You must be Kryssi."

"You must be my daddy," said Kryssi. "I read the letter my mommy wrote to Aunt Piper. I know she's not my aunt, but it didn't seem respectful to just call her Piper."

Rodney was speechless again. She was carrying on a conversation like a child of ten or so. Yet physically, she couldn't have been three yet.

"There you are! You tricked me again!" Piper returned from her search. Kryssi giggled the way a toddler should have. She was a contradiction; much like Rodney himself.

"Are you going to take me away," Kryssi asked. Her innocent eyes stared up at Rodney and he would not have been able to refuse her anything.

"That is not my plan," he said. "There are a lot of things that have to be arranged before any decisions of that kind can be made. Piper breathed a nearly imperceptible sigh of relief. She loved Kryssi and didn't want to lose her.

"But I will visit a lot," he said. "If that's okay with you."

"Please, please, PLEASE!" Rodney's eyes widened. Her enthusiasm was so sudden and unsolicited.

"I promise," he said. "I have to go arrange to have some tests done and then I will visit often."

"Tests like mommy?" There was a sudden sadness in her eyes that was very mature for her age.

"Maybe," said Rodney. "I don't know yet. I will tell you about it when I come back."

"Okay," she said. "Bye!" Kryssi ran down the hall as carefree as a toddler should be.

"That was quick," he said.

"I think she might have a bit of an attention deficit," said Piper.

"Maybe," said Rodney. "Time will tell I guess."

"I am sure it will," said Piper.

"I should get going. I have a lot of things to think about and some arrangements to make." He extended his hand to Piper. She ignored it and embraced him fully. "You're family now," she said. He hugged her back and left before he began to cry.

Rodney's life had never been what he expected. A person feels as though nothing will ever surprise them again when they get to a certain age and Rodney had felt that way. Life had other plans. Maybe Daphne had stacked the deck in his case, but he was going to take those treatments. Rodney was confident that he was going to live at least another fifty years; maybe a hundred. No one could say. He had faith in Daphne's research and he had a daughter now. His goal would be live long enough to fulfill Daphne's wishes and legacy. Rodney realized that for the first time in his life, he was actually glad to be alive.

-END-

The More Things Change...

It had never been Albert's intention to stay in one place very long. He had had all he wanted of staying put during the twelve years he attended public school. Thirteen, if you counted kindergarten. Albert got the job as dishwasher at the 71st Street Diner while he was in his senior year of high school. He saved his money so he could take a trip to Europe, but used it instead to go to college. His grades were nothing to crow about, but the community college at the time had pretty lenient standards. He worked hard, both at his studies and his job, but college wasn't a good fit for him. Perhaps if he had gone to one of the big-named universities and stayed in a dorm, he might have found college more exciting and the classes more interesting; more challenging. As it was, he found college nothing to be more than additional learning of things he already knew or would never use. Albert dropped out during the first semester of his second year. He regretted not dropping out sooner, so that at least he would get a partial refund of his tuition, but he chalked it up to an *unlearning* experience.

Quitting college meant that Albert could work full-time at the diner. His duties expanded to include busing tables and filling in for the short-order cook from time to time. The diner paid him just enough so that he couldn't afford to quit, but not enough to let him realize his dreams of traveling the world. Maybe if he had been able to cook full-time, things might have been different; but the regular guy wasn't going anywhere for the time being. Neither was Albert, it seemed.

The diner was never that busy, but always seemed to make money. The business model ran contrary to everything Albert had been taught in his college economics course. He had a lot of free time between dish loads and busing to observe the customers. *How interesting their lives must be*, thought Albert. He made up exciting back stories that suited them when he thought their lives seemed too dull to be interesting. He sat in the back booth when the owner wasn't there and pretended to read a paperback. The stories he deduced or flat-out made up were far more interesting than what he was usually reading.

It was 1973 when Albert first came to work at the diner. In the mid-seventies, he started full-time when he quit college. The Vietnam War had ended without requiring his participation. He would have gone if called to duty, but he wasn't too enthusiastic about volunteering. The economy went south after the Watergate scandal, so keeping his job was more important than ever.

The diner allowed Albert to observe all facets of society and see how they interconnected. Middle-management business executives would lunch on BLTs and coffee while they would discuss accounts or new additions to the secretarial pool. They would come in groups of two or more and make sure everyone paid their own check for tax purposes. They always wanted receipts. Women who worked at the same companies usually had salads because image was everything. The gender double standard was extremely prevalent back then. The women usually dined alone.

Hippies still showed up on a regular basis, even though the news media no longer seemed to consider them relevant. They often wore macramé belts, beads and bellbottoms, just as one would expect. One hippy named Syd wore a brown rawhide vest, which had been sliced around the bottom to make fringe; and elephant-hide sandals...even in winter. He seemed to have a different *old lady* with him every couple of weeks or so. He was also alone a lot. Syd used to talk to Albert when he was busing his table; Albert would stop to listen because he made a lot of sense. Syd was also usually high as a kite and Albert found that amusing.

"I'm a conundrum," Syd would say. "I am a free spirit who yearns to be tied down. I want a woman by my side…but who will stay the hell away from me for her own good."

"Keep looking," replied Albert. "You'll find the right one someday."

"I already did," said Syd. "…but she'd already found somebody else." Tears formed in his eyes. Albert pretended not to notice and finished busing his table. "Things will work out," he offered. He wasn't sure if his words were of any comfort.

"Maybe in the next life," Syd remarked. He would usually sit at the table for a few more minutes and then leave when Albert wasn't looking; as though he had simply evaporated.

A string of fads punctuated the end of the Seventies and the early Eighties. Disco ushered in Roller Disco. That was replaced by the *cowboy boot* and *belt buckle* trend. Urban cowboys line danced as lighted disco floors were torn up and mechanical bulls were installed. The hippies stepped back into the shadows for a while and the yuppies took the spotlight. Pastels replaced tie-dye. Albert marveled at how fast everything changed in the world around him. Progress had sped by like a subway train at five o'clock, but his job and the 71st Street Diner resisted the change. It had remained pretty much the same as it always had; the same menus, the same patrons, the same conversations, day in and day out. It was true that the more things changed, the more everything stayed the same, as the saying goes. Albert didn't notice middle age creeping up on him. He thought there was something he ought to be accomplishing, but he had no idea what. So he kept washing dishes and waiting for that big thing to happen, whatever it was going to be. Deep inside, he knew that nothing was ever going to change.

Walking into the 71st Street Diner was like stepping back in time, except for the prices. A piece of pie was now $1.75 instead of a quarter; but the atmosphere was still the same. Most restaurants had eliminated dishwashers and converted to automatic dishwashers which steamed and sterilized dishes. But the 71st Street Diner held onto tradition and tried to maintain its authenticity and charm in a modern world. Chrome, stainless steel and red vinyl still decorated the dining area; and the antique fixtures that were new when the diner was built added to the charm and nostalgia. Gleaming stainless steel appliances, terra cotta tile and metal shelving decorated the kitchen. Only the modern cash register risked shattering the illusion but the customers were content to suspend their disbelief. One might expect the men to be wearing gray flannel suits and felt fedoras as they dined. It would be easy to imagine women wearing tight, but fashionable dresses with jackets and pillbox hats. Then, just as sudden as turning on a light switch, everything changed.

In the Eighties, the economy became unstable and the diner changed hands. The original owner was sorry to let it go, but his health had begun to fail and he needed a warmer climate. The new owners were more about making money than keeping a *historic* landmark of the community. The neighborhood wasn't happy when they expanded the diner to annex the vacant lot next to it and converted it into a bar; but they soon got over it. Albert was able to stay on as kitchen help and his job description expanded to include the title of part-time bartender. He found that the position suited him perfectly. The regular bartender worked most of the busy shifts because the tips were better. Albert got to work the off-hours when business was slow, but he could continue to observe the clientele.

The new owners turned out to be absentee employers. As long as the money kept coming in, they didn't really care how the business was run. The bar was mainly used for tax deduction purposes anyway. That lack of supervision led to a bit of shady business taking place in the dark corners of the bar. Drugs occasionally changed hands in the corner booth where Albert used to read and people watch. Prostitutes occasionally came to the bar, but never to conduct business. There wasn't any money in it for them there. They mostly came because the bar was a temporary haven from their lives on the streets. The classic look of the décor allowed them to pretend they lived in a simpler time and, for a little while, be someone other than who they were. Albert didn't even recognize them as hookers in the beginning.

They liked being treated as ordinary people and not being judged.

All in all, the patrons of the bar were pretty well-behaved. Bikers became frequent customers, but not so much as to call it a biker bar. The bar even sponsored charity rides and chili cook-offs a couple of times a year. One of the more colorful bikers was a guy named Ed or Eddie. Most people just called him Buck because of his fringed buckskin biker jacket. He was, as he himself used to say, "…long in the tooth and as rough as the road." He liked to hit on girls who were thirty or so years younger than he was. Most thought he was cute, but didn't take him seriously. Some thought he was annoying and drove him away. He did get lucky a few times; or so he said. No one wanted to call him a liar because they liked him and didn't want to make him angry. Besides, he might have been telling the truth and no one wanted to hear the details if he was.

Another regular was Mark. He was a contractor by day. In the evenings, he was a regular at the pool tables. He was pretty good, but not so good that he ever made any money. No one ever tried to roll him in the parking lot anyway. It didn't hurt that he travelled with about six or seven friends all the time. There was a party wherever Mark went because he was the one who brought it. He made friends with whoever was in the bar at the time and didn't seem to have an enemy in the world. That was what Albert thought anyway. Albert also thought that Mark's gregarious nature might be concealing pain and regret. But then, who wasn't?

Albert's own pain came in the form of betrayal. Rejection bothered him, to be sure; but he was used to that. He wasn't a rock star or a bodybuilder. He started out average-looking and got less average as he aged. Albert seemed to always attract or be attracted to the wrong kind of women. The ones who had way too much emotional baggage. He tried to help in any way that he could, but they didn't want help. The princesses didn't want to be rescued from the dragons that held them captive. His relationships ended with the princesses resenting him for his efforts and making his life miserable for it.

Gwen was his most difficult relationship to date. She was pretty in an understated kind of way with a deadly combination of self-entitlement and low self-esteem. Albert wasn't sure how those two traits could bond together in the same person. She had confessed to him that she suffered from bipolar disorder, but she wore the title on her sleeve like a badge of honor and refused counseling or medication. Instead, she played the bipolar card when she just wanted to have things her way, blow off steam or blame someone else for her problems. No one dared call her out on her behavior and so there were never any immediate consequences for her actions. Thus, she had no reason to change or to seek help. Albert took all the abuse he could before he finally ended the relationship.

The very next night, Gwen showed up at the bar. He thought she was going to flirt with every guy there, but she zeroed in on only one; Ashton Dell III. He was a high school assistant gym coach and a bully. His toadies called him Trey. He didn't have any actual friends and he didn't really want any. Instead, he liked having minions who simply enforced his will, and women only served one purpose for him. Trey could have been a success in almost anything he studied for, but it was easier to bully others into doing his homework. That trend continued into college. After two years, he had enough credits to get a teaching credential and bullied his way into a job that didn't require a lot of effort.

Trey and Albert had a conflict a few months before in a bar on the edge of town. Albert had been there to meet a friend when Trey picked a fight with him. Albert's friend wasn't there and Trey had two burly thugs with him. He wasn't a fighter and he didn't want to go to jail, so he didn't resist and left the bar with his figurative tail between his legs. It seemed as if the entire bar laughed at him as he left. Maybe they were. Gwen had seemed to understand when he told her about it, but actually she filed in away in her head to use on Albert at a later date.

The night Gwen zeroed in on Trey they immediately got out on the dancefloor. Albert knew that Gwen's suggestive presentation was to entice Trey but was directed at him. He felt like the entire bar was laughing at him again. He pretended not to watch and casually tended bar. When Trey's hands dropped to caress Gwen's butt, Albert felt as though his heart was collapsing in on itself. His face flushed and his mouth got very dry. It wasn't that he had feelings for Gwen (except contempt). It was that she was with Albert's sworn enemy. That made his chest burn and his stomach churn. She realized he was looking at them and she made a point of sticking her tongue in Trey's mouth. Shaken, he dropped a bottle of expensive Irish whiskey and it shattered. Immediately, the catcalls came from all over the bar. *Cut him off! That's coming out of your check! You're fired!* The whole bar really was laughing at him then and he came very close to quitting that night. He didn't though. That would be exactly what Gwen wanted. Albert was tougher than that.

That night impacted Albert more than he let anyone know. His weight fluctuated between *you've put on a few pounds and are you getting enough to eat?* Working in a diner/bar was not conducive to maintaining a healthy diet. The food was prepared two ways; fried and deep fried. The oven was only used for pizza. He tried bringing his own lunch, but the aroma of the decadent breaded fare was too much for him to resist. He tried eating smaller portions but caved in a lot.

Albert also enjoyed his beer. That didn't help him control his weight. Occasionally, he would participate in a round of shots and very rarely he would have a Scotch straight up; but mostly he just drank beer. He tried some of the beers with lower calories and carbs, but they tasted weak and had lower alcohol contents. Albert just ended up drinking more of them to compensate for their lack of taste and his lack of a buzz. Eventually he went back to his regular brew.

A few years after the Gwen incident, karma caught up with Trey. He made the news statewide when he was accused and later convicted of sexually assaulting three high school cheerleaders. Only one of them was female. Other students came forward after that and Trey's career was over; as was his life outside prison walls for the next decade or so. Albert felt it was a hollow victory, but a victory nonetheless. He thought about Gwen when he heard the news, but he never saw her again. That was probably for the best. He hoped she was happy in spite of her treatment of him. Albert didn't want anyone to be unhappy ever, except maybe for Trey.

Albert's life wasn't exciting, but it wasn't necessarily dull. He didn't get to travel the world, but if he waited long enough the world came to him. His town wasn't large, but the state capital wasn't very far away; so it picked up the overflow from sold-out sporting events and concerts from time to time. People from all over the country and the world drifted in to sample the bar's menu and ambience. Albert waited on them all as if they were regulars. He got used to the fact that the Europeans didn't tip and that they weren't trying to insult him. Tipping just wasn't embedded in their cultures.

A pileup on the interstate brought an entire busload of people into the bar one evening. They ended up missing the regional finals and had to be content with watching the game on the big screens in the bar. The crowd consoled themselves by reminding themselves that the beer was at least cheaper than it was at the stadium. This was a small consolation, considering they were nearly all season ticket holders. Those who supported the winning team tipped big that night and those of the losing team drank big. In the end, everyone cancelled their hotel reservations and the bus headed back the way it had come.

The name of the bar was changed again in the nineties. It became the 71st Street Bar & Grill. It wasn't much of a change, but it afforded the owners to spring for a new neon sign and apply for another round of tax breaks. Albert didn't know the details of such stuff. He just kept tending bar and people watching. By that time, he was the full-time bartender on the evening shift. The new neon sign attracted the wrong type of people to begin with and Albert got robbed three days after the grand opening. It was a quick robbery and the robber was as nervous as Albert was. It was early in the shift, so there wasn't a lot of money in the till. Still, it shook him up. He had never been robbed before and wasn't quite sure how to handle it.

Albert did better the next couple of times he was robbed. He just pointed to the red light flashing on the device on the wall and remarked, "See that light? That is the security camera. The flashing light signifies that the silent alarm has been tripped. You have less than three minutes to get out of here."

"Hand over the money then!" the thief demanded.

"I would like to do that," said Albert. "…but I have to enter my code to get into the cash register and if I mess up, it will lock me out until the owner comes in to override it. Please don't shoot." Albert wasn't really worried. The robber had his hand in the pocket of his hoodie and threatened him with an indication that he had a gun. By the look of the rounded protrusion in the fabric, Albert was pretty sure it was the thief's finger. If it wasn't his finger, he must have been *really happy* to see Albert.

The bandit finally fled on foot, empty-handed so to speak. Albert smiled at Mark, who had witnessed the whole event.

"Can you believe he tried to bluff me with his finger?" Albert asked.

"I can't believe that he couldn't tell the difference between a security camera and a smoke detector," answered Mark. "When are you going to change the battery in that thing?"

"I might not change it now," replied Albert. "I think it works better as a robbery deterrent."

"Maybe," said Mark. "Hey, can I get some change for the pool table?"

"Sure thing," Albert said. He opened the cash register and exchanged three dollars in quarters for three crisp one dollar bills.

"I thought you had to enter a security code for that to open," said Mark.

"I also said the smoke detector was a security camera," Albert responded.

"They do not pay you enough," declared Mark.

"You're preaching to the choir brother," Albert agreed. The rest of the night was pretty quiet but pleasant.

Seasons passed. Some old regulars moved on. Other old-timers passed away. New customers took their places and blended seamlessly in with the remaining old regulars. Albert became the fixed point in a changing world, much like the bar. A party on New Year's Eve ushered in the new millennium.

Albert got depressed. The year 2000 arrived and he didn't have a dime more saved than he did twenty years before. His plan in the eighties had been to start a retirement account. He never got around to it. Instead, his investment strategy consisted of spending five dollars a week on lottery tickets and diversifying his portfolio by spending a couple of dollars on scratch-offs. The most he ever won was just enough to dine on prime rib once in a while...for one. He was pretty sure he was going to have to work at the bar until he died.

Albert never listened to the news if he could help it. There was enough drama going on in life in general without adding commentary to it. Plus, he didn't trust the news since it sold advertising. It didn't feel objective anymore. That is why he didn't know anything about the destruction of the World Trade Center on September 11th until he came to work on that Tuesday afternoon. The bar was like a bedridden patient on that day; depressed and silent. For the most part, people sat staring at the television screens in wide-eyed disbelief as the news outlets played the captured video footage over and over. Sometimes an argument would erupt out of nowhere and then settle back down. Theories were abundant and varied.

"I blame the Russians," one would say.

"It's not the Russians," another would counter. "They would have just nuked us."

"You're both wrong," a third interjected. "The President knew about the whole thing beforehand. I never did trust that little..."

"It doesn't matter who's to blame," shouted Miller Craig. He was a retired school teacher and used to calming down unruly students. "We need to focus on the fact that people lost their lives. Their families and loved ones need our concern. We don't need to fight amongst ourselves." There was more than one red face in the bar after he made his statement. Everyone quieted down and went back to drinking and staring at the television.

Albert was concerned for the families, but the event also got him thinking about his own mortality. He wondered what it would have been like if he had been in one of those towers and considered what he would have to show for his life. He had a half-brother out west, but they hadn't spoken for eight years or so. There would be no one to miss him; no one would mourn at Albert's graveside. He wouldn't even *have* a graveside. He didn't have a pre-arranged funeral or any family to speak of. The patrons of the bar would miss him for a while. They would reminisce about him fondly and maybe play a song on the jukebox in his honor, but they would move on. The world would too. It always does.

The skies were empty for a few days after September 11th. Airlines had grounded their fleets to step-up security measures. Albert decided that maybe life was too short to delay doing what he wanted to do. His full-time bartender position had allowed him to put some money back for a change. Once the planes began to fly again, he booked a flight to the west coast. His excuse was to reestablish contact with his half-brother who lived in Eugene Oregon; but mostly he wanted to see the Pacific Ocean at least once before he died.

Albert's flight was scheduled just two and a half weeks after the attack on the World Trade Center. He had never flown before, commercially or otherwise, but could tell that there was more tension in the air than usual. His seat was by the window and just ahead of the right wing. He tensed up when he heard and felt two successive thumps under his feet. A lady next to him placed her hand on his arm and whispered, "Don't worry; that was just the landing gear coming up. It will do the same thing before we land. You want it to make that noise."

Albert thanked her and looked out the window as the ground dropped away. He wasn't afraid of heights, but he really hated not being in control of the movement. He was a bit of a control freak. Every time the plane banked, Albert would lean the opposite way to try to right it. By the third time he leaned into the lady next to him, she was getting a little annoyed, but she was also amused.

"You know that the plane is not going to respond to you shifting your weight, right?"

"I know," Albert answered. "I apologize. I can't seem to help it. It's my first flight…but I guess you knew that already."

"I was pretty sure," she replied. "My name is Jessica."

"Albert," he offered. "I am sorry to be a bother."

"Don't worry about it," said Jessica. "Usually these flights are pretty boring…even with the movie."

"There's a movie?" asked Albert. He sounded like a little kid.

"Yes," responded Jessica. "The screens will drop down in a few minutes. Probably right after the fight attendants get drinks and pretzels for us."

"No nuts?" Albert had always heard that they served nuts on flights.

"Not anymore," said Jessica. "I guess too many people were allergic. Personally, I think it is just cheaper to serve pretzels."

Albert couldn't help but like Jessica. She was about his age, but she didn't look it. Her eyes were the same color as her sandy brown hair and her skin indicated that she got some sun; but not too much sun.

"Since this is your first flight," she announced, "…I am going to buy you a drink."

"You don't have to do that," said Albert.

"I insist," asserted Jessica.

"Okay," agreed Albert. "I guess I could use a beer." The flight attendant came by with his drink cart. His badge indicated his name was Stuart.

"Stuart," said Jessica, "We would like two beers please…and two shots of your finest whiskey." Albert's eyes opened wide.

"Are those both for you?" Albert asked.

"Nope," she said. "I have to tell you something and you are probably going to need this."

"You're not pregnant, are you?"

"Would I be drinking if I was pregnant?" she asked, smiling. "You silly goose."

"Sorry," replied Albert. He had a wide nervous grin. "Occupational hazard."

"Really? What do you do?"

"I am a bartender, if you can believe that," Albert answered.

"How ironic," said Jessica. "…and here I am serving you drinks."

"Technically, I am serving the drinks," Stuart interjected, smiling. "That will be sixteen dollars."

"Sixteen dollars!" exclaimed Albert.

"This isn't the sixties," said Jessica. "Here, Stuart. Keep the change." She handed him a twenty. "...and don't be a stranger. I think my friend is going to need a booster shot in a few minutes."

"Well," added Stuart. "...just as long as your friend doesn't get too rowdy. I might need to cut back on his medication."

"He'll be fine," said Jessica. "I will keep him under control." Stuart winked at her and moved on down the aisle. Albert looked at Jessica quizzically.

"What is it you are going to tell me about that I need this?" he asked.

"First we drink," said Jessica. She poured half a beer into each plastic cup and then half a shot into them.

"I don't know too many girls who drink Boilermakers," said Albert. "...and I'm a bartender."

"These got me through the tough times," said Jessica. "I first tried them in college. Good times!" Albert gave her a look of admiration, took a sip and winced. He wasn't used to beer mixed with hard alcohol or with attractive women being so affable to him.

"You're doing it wrong," she said. "You have to chug the first one." She turned up her cup and downed the drink. Albert did likewise. She was right. It wasn't so bad when he did it like that. The whisky gave him the usual warm feeling in the pit of his stomach he got when he occasionally drank scotch. He liked it. After a moment or two, he relaxed. The movie screens came down and the flight attendants went down the aisle distributing headphones.

"I think I am relaxed now," said Albert. "What do you have to tell me?"

"I figured I should tell you instead of you hearing it when you are not prepared," she stated softly. "This 737 is the same type of plane that was hijacked in the World Trade Center attacks." Albert looked around the cabin and tried to imagine what the passengers of those ill-fated flights must have gone through. He pictured them making their final calls to their families, as well as the dread and panic they must have felt. He poured his second boilermaker himself and downed it without hesitation.

"The next round is on me," he offered.

"Easy cowboy," replied Jessica. "This is a long flight and you haven't experienced turbulence yet." Albert smiled. It had been a long time since someone had seemed to care about his well-being. And he liked it when she called him *cowboy*. The way she said it was sexy and Albert thought she seemed to be flirting. That puzzled him because she was, in his opinion, way out of his league.

The luxurious airline meal consisted of a *po' boy* submarine and a bag of chips. The sandwich was only slightly more flavorful than the plastic it came wrapped in. Albert paired it with another boilermaker. He had a significant buzz by the time the movie started. It was a romantic comedy and starred an actress whose name Albert could never pronounce correctly. By halfway through the movie, he and Jessica had their fingers clasped together. It was partly because of the movie and partly because of the alcohol; but mostly it was because neither of them had watched a movie with anyone in a long time and it just felt right. Albert felt like he was in high school again. Only this time, he had a hot girlfriend and he was popular; in his mind anyway. The flight experienced a lot of turbulence over the mountains, but Albert hardly noticed.

What he did notice was the fighter jet which escorted the plane into Seattle. That made him uneasy. Albert knew enough to be aware that Seattle was probably a potential terrorist target. All of the nation's landmarks were. What he found the most disquieting though was that his life was now in the steady or unsteady hands of the pilot he hadn't even seen. He was about to order another boilermaker, but Jessica placed her hand softly on his arm and shook her head. Albert smiled at her and thought that it was probably for the best. He really didn't need it. Besides, it seemed like the restrooms were always occupied and he didn't need to put any additional pressure on his bladder.

The plane was able to land without the fighter jet escort shooting it down, so life went on. Albert and Jessica had become so close during the flight that they looked like they had always been a couple as they debarked from the plane. They proceeded to the luggage carousel and they waited for their luggage to arrive. There was an awkward silence as Albert tried to think of something to say that didn't sound like a cheesy line. Jessica spared him the discomfort by speaking first.

"I don't want to be forward," she began. "...but I like you, Albert. I have a sense about people and I can tell you are a nice guy."

"Thank you," replied Albert. "I don't think you are being forward at all. I like you too...a lot."

"The problem is, I live here and you live two thousand miles away."

"I know," said Albert. He felt dejected and was sure she was trying to let him down easy. His defenses kicked in and he began to ramble.

"I could quit my job," he stammered. "I don't have anything keeping me in the Midwest; not really." He regretted how desperate he sounded halfway through his sentence, but it was too late to turn back.

"I don't want you to quit your job," said Jessica. "This feels like a sudden impulse and do not usually make impulsive decisions. I don't think we should make any life-altering plans based on a single plane ride."

"I agree," said Albert. He swallowed a hard lump in his throat. "...but we shouldn't take this too lightly either. If the terrorist attack has taught us anything, it's that life is short; life is precious and there is no guarantee of a future."

"Why does that sound like something from a movie?" asked Jessica. She raised an eyebrow and smiled.

"Did you like that?" asked Albert. "I just made it up. I can do it with a Humphrey Bogart voice if that would help."

"I think it belongs on a t-shirt or a greeting card," answered Jessica. "I think you missed your calling."

"I have a crazy idea," said Albert. He paused for a long time and prepared for rejection. "I have a rental car reserved. I planned to drive down the coast of Washington and then most of the way on the coast to Eugene Oregon. Why don't you come with me? You could show me the sights and we could just see where things lead." He looked hopeful and rejected at the same time. The prolonged pause Jessica took didn't fill him with confidence.

"Do you think I can just pick up and leave whenever I want?" asked Jessica. There was a touch of indignation in her voice.

"I'm sorry," said Albert. "I just got so excited, I didn't think."

"I'm kidding," Jessica replied. "I can pick up and leave whenever I want. I'm the boss."

"Really? I feel so inconsiderate for not asking what you did for a living." Albert apologized a few more times.

"I don't usually volunteer the information to anyone," said Jessica. "I have a software company that is pretty successful. I can manage it from anywhere in the world as long as I can connect to the internet. I don't usually tell people what I do because they treat me differently. They begin to act like I am looking down on them. I am taking a big chance with you. I hope you know that."

"Actually, you having money makes no difference to me," Albert maintained. "I have never had any great aspirations; I've always been just what I am. People are just people. I'm just glad you are free to do what you want."

"Good," Jessica whispered. She leaned over and kissed Albert on the cheek. He felt a surge of electricity when her lips touched his face. He hadn't felt anything like that for a very long time; maybe never. A loud buzzer sounded and the luggage carousel started with a lurch. They both jumped as did. It made several rotations before the first piece of luggage arrived. No one was there to claim it and Albert thought that was a little odd.

"I think the person that belongs to is probably waiting at a carousel in Boise," said Jessica. "To bad. He would have been first."

It took Albert a moment before Jessica's statement struck him. He began to laugh in a way that some might have considered maniacal. Jessica didn't think the joke was that funny, but seeing Albert so amused made her laugh. They continued to laugh each time a suitcase fell through the conveyor door. People thought they were a little crazy. Airport security was watching them closely until they left.

The two eventually collected all their bags and proceeded to the rental car counter. There, Albert picked up the keys to the car he pre-ordered…a white sport convertible. He wondered why a convertible had been available. Then it began to rain as they crossed the lot to where the car was parked and he understood. *Oh well*, he thought. *At least it's a sports car.*

The Washington coast was rocky and the ocean was brilliant shade of blue. Whitecaps formed irregular yet consistent patterns as the surf crashed on the rocky coastline. An hour into their journey south, the sun came out and Albert put the top down. Jessica tied her long sandy brown hair up with a scarf and

Albert felt as though they were in a movie. Try as he did, he couldn't come up with another catchy line to impress Jessica, but she didn't need to be impressed. She loved the ride and she didn't get a pressuring vibe from Albert at all.

The drive from Seattle to Eugene was took six hours with a few stops for gas and bathroom breaks. Albert got a little hoarse from trying to talk over the wind and stopped at a convenience store just before they crossed the bridge to Portland. He bought a lottery ticket and cough lozenges. He bought another ticket once they crossed into Oregon.

"It's part of my investment portfolio," explained Albert.

"Part of your five-year plan?" jabbed Jessica.

"Yes," said Albert. "I will buy these for the next five years or until I die; whichever comes first."

"Don't say that," Jessica replied. She choked back some tears. Albert was surprised by her reaction. At first he thought she was joking. He never had someone care that much about him…especially after only knowing him such a short time. It touched him deeply.

"I'm sorry," he said. "I guess I never really felt like it mattered much whether I lived or died before."

"Actually," said Jessica. "I'm sorry. I kind of overreacted. I lost my dad a couple of years ago and it still hurts a bit. I miss him a lot sometimes."

"I am really sorry," said Albert. "I promise; no more talk of death for the rest of the trip."

"I will hold you to that," she said.

"I expect you to," said Albert. "I do not make promises lightly."

They drove west to the coast from Portland before heading south. Neither of them talked much. Albert's throat still hurt and he didn't want to swallow a cough lozenge. They stopped in Cannon Beach and ate dinner at a seaside restaurant. The couple put their arms around each other as they watched the sun go down. Jessica was sure that their silhouettes against the backdrop of the orange sunset would make an awesome screensaver. A few tourists probably agreed and took their picture without their knowledge; probably to use as wallpaper on their own computer screens. The best picture was when they kissed. The setting sun between them and looked like a spark of magic where their lips met.

Eugene Oregon was another three hours away and jetlag was taking its toll on the couple. Albert pulled into a gas station on an isolated part of the highway to ask where they might find a motel for the night. He was willing to sleep in the car if need be.

As he opened the glass door, he froze. A small man in a ski mask looked at him from behind the counter.

"Don't move!" he shouted nervously.

"I'm not going anywhere," said Albert calmly. "I just need directions." From behind the counter, Albert heard a pitiful whimper.

"Shut up!" yelled the man in the mask.

"You should probably hurry," remarked Albert.

"What?"

"You see that flashing light up there," asked Albert? "That means a silent alarm has been triggered. You should get out of here as quickly as possible."

"Not until I get in the safe," sneered the thief.

"They don't let the night guy have the combination to the safe," explained Albert. "I should know. You probably only have a minute. I don't know how sound travels out here, but I think I hear a siren. I'm from back east, so I can't really tell."

The man looked out the door and down to the safe. He ran his tongue across his lips and decided not to take any chances. He took the thirty dollars from the cash register, bolted past Albert and disappeared into the night.

"It's okay," said Albert. "You can get up now."

"That was incredible!" exclaimed the attendant. "You stayed so calm."

"Not really," Albert responded. "You don't sell dry pants by any chance?" The shaken attendant smiled.

"Anything you want," he said. "...take it. I will cover it."

"That's not necessary," replied Albert. "I just need directions to a motel or someplace where I can crash for the night."

"There's no motel around here," the attendant answered. "...but there is a bed and breakfast about three miles north. You have to look very carefully for the sign, but it is almost on the beach."

"That's perfect," said Albert. "Oh, and you might want to change the batteries in your smoke detector. Safety first, you know." He headed back to the car, stopped and went back.

"One more thing," he said. "I need a lottery ticket."

The bed and breakfast was perfect. Albert and Jessica slept together, but only slept. They were so tired and the sound of the surf gently lapping the shore was hypnotic and lulled them to sleep. A romantic, nearly full moon reflecting on the ocean was lost on them. They slept peacefully and were awakened by heavier waves crashing on the beach and rocks as the tide came in. Both of them opened their eyes at the same time and smiled. Then there was a mutual look of horror. They each covered their mouths at the same time, afraid the other would detect the awful morning breath they both knew they had.

After the breakfast part of their bed and breakfast adventure, they were back on the road heading south. They learned a lot about each other on the journey. Albert's half-brother Denver met them on the outskirts of Eugene so they could follow him to his house.

"Not that I am complaining," Denver said, "…but I didn't know you were bringing a guest."

"This is Jessica," explained Albert. "We met on the plane."

"It's very nice to meet you," Denver said. Then he leaned in, smiled and softly suggested, "If he's holding you hostage, blink twice."

"That will be enough of that," admonished Albert. "Besides, we're on high alert right now. That kind of talk could get someone in trouble."

"Yeah… you," countered Denver. "Okay, I'll be good. If you're ready, follow me."

It was a good thing that Denver led them to his house because Albert could not have followed the twists and turns which were on the directions Denver had sent. Denver led them to a roomy but modest home surrounded by tall fir trees.

"I hope you like spaghetti," he offered when they arrived. "Betty does the best job on it."

"Spaghetti for lunch," said Albert. "Sounds great."

"I can read that tone," claimed Denver. "The only spaghetti you are used to comes out of a can, for lunch or otherwise. You probably have it for breakfast too." Albert couldn't argue.

The spaghetti they had was not the spaghetti Albert was used to. It was made with angel hair pasta and was tossed in olive oil, diced tomatoes, garlic and mushrooms. He ate it, but he would have preferred something with a nice marinara sauce. Jessica really enjoyed hers.

Dinner was a little more to Albert's liking. Denver made steaks out on the grill. Betty baked potatoes and Jessica helped with the tossed salad. Afterwards, they all sat around a fire in the chiminea, drank a fine Washington state wine and looked up at an incredible blanket of stars.

"When are you moving out here?" asked Denver.

"What makes you think I want to move out here?" Albert felt a little ambushed.

"Everybody who visits wants to stay," answered Denver. "Besides, what have you got back east that keeps you there?" Albert looked over at Jessica. The glow of the fire on her soft features gave him a warm feeling inside.

"Nothing really, I guess," he said absently.

Albert only stayed two days with his half-brother. There was a lot he wanted to see and not a lot of time to see it. He bid Denver goodbye and promised he would make another visit soon. He and Jessica finally found their way back to the highway after a couple of wrong turns and continued to travel south. Albert wanted to see the giant redwoods and Sequoias in California. They were on his bucket list. He was glad he had someone to share the trip with and so was Jessica. She had never seen them even though she lived much closer to them than Albert did. She had been too busy shaping her business.

Time seemed to crawl at the beginning of the trip and then sped up to light speed toward its end. They made their way back to Seattle, staying overnight at the same bed and breakfast they had stayed at before. This time, they didn't just sleep and the moonlight on the ocean wasn't lost on them. The next morning they endured each other's morning breath for a long, passionate good morning kiss. That might not have been all they did that morning. Then they showered, dressed and went down to breakfast. The lady that ran the bed and breakfast gave them a knowing look, embarrassing them a bit. They got back on the road and were silent most of the trip. It wasn't that they had run out of things to say. It was that they were afraid they would choke up if they tried to talk.

When Albert and Jessica said goodbye at the airport, both of them felt as though their hearts were being ripped from their chests. Albert tried to hide his pain but Jessica expressed hers fully. Albert promised he would keep in touch by phone and on his computer. Jessica said she would hold him to that.

"I don't make promises I don't keep," he said. They kissed for a long time and Jessica watched as Albert headed down the boarding ramp to the plane. She wondered if she would ever see him again.

Albert sat silently for most of the trip home. He looked for Stuart on the flight, but thought that would be the most extraordinary coincidence if he had been. The movie on the flight was another romantic comedy, but it didn't seem funny since he was going home alone. He felt the now-familiar thump of the landing gear and a tear formed in the corner of his eye as he thought once again of Jessica.

Albert returned to his job as a bartender and settled back into his routine. The bar seemed less like a place the world came to now and more like a prison keeping him locked away from it. His stomach churned whenever someone ordered a boilermaker. He felt trapped in his job for the first time in his life. He didn't want to stay, but he didn't have the money to go anywhere. The trip to Oregon had taken every dime of his life savings. He suspected that Jessica would pay for another trip if he asked her, but he wasn't going to use her like that. If he lost respect for himself, he wouldn't be the man she wanted. That was the logic he used anyway.

Albert was about to give up on the idea of ever getting to go back out west when a package arrived for him at the bar. He usually had his mail sent to the bar because he didn't trust the neighbors in his apartment building. The return address was Seattle and his heart jumped a little when he read it. Inside the 14 by 18-inch box was another box and a greeting card. In the card, Jessica wrote: You have no excuse for not keeping in touch with me now. Contact me soon and enjoy. Love (that's right…I said it!) Jessica.

Albert looked over his shoulder to see if anyone else had read his card. The bar was nearly empty except for Mark and a few other guys he didn't know. He opened the inner box and found a state-of-the-art laptop which he could have never afforded. A note stuck to it gave him Jessica's email address. Albert wasted no time hooking it up to the phone line. He opened his own email account and nervously typed a message. He composed it three times before actually sending it. The first two attempts sounded desperate and mushy. That wasn't how he wanted to sound.

A response to his message came a mere fifteen minutes later. Jessica was thrilled that he had received her gift. She was a little afraid that she would seem too pushy. Albert didn't feel that way at all; although he did feel a little inadequate. Jessica didn't push and seemed very content to continue with their relationship being long-distance. She sent him a cellphone with unlimited minutes and called it a 'business expense'. Albert would have protested, but he wanted to hear her voice again and he really appreciated her generosity. Besides, if she was as successful as she said, she could probably afford it.

Albert waited until his shift was over before calling Jessica. He was so excited when she answered that he talked with her until his battery ran down. Then he plugged it in and talked to her until morning. They never seemed to run out of things to talk about. Albert felt he finally did have something to live for and look forward to; even if it was just electronic communication with someone more than two thousand miles away.

Thanks to being able to keep in contact with Jessica, Albert was content to settle back into his old routine. He gained enough confidence to demand a raise and was surprised when he got it without question. He wondered why he hadn't ask for one sooner. He also wondered why he didn't ask for more money. Albert opened a program on his new laptop and started to do a serious budget plan. He wanted to manage his money in a way that he could make at least two trips a year to the West Coast. Although he might have to give up his weekly lottery investment plan to make it work.

That reminded him of something. Albert took out his wallet and looked at the lottery tickets he bought while he was with Jessica. He exited out of his finance program and connected to the internet. He opened the site for the Washington State lottery and looked up the winning numbers for the date on his ticket. He read the winning numbers out loud, alternating between the numbers that had been drawn and the numbers on his ticket.

Seventeen...(twelve)...Nineteen...(twenty-two)...Thirty-four...(thirty-three). None of the other numbers matched. It didn't matter. He set the ticket aside. It was going into a scrapbook of his trip when he made one.

He opened up the page for the Oregon lottery and began checking his other numbers.

Five...(nine)...Eighteen...(EIGHTEEN!)...Twenty-eight...(thirty)...Thirty-one...(thirty-five)...Thirty-nine...(forty-one)...Forty-four...(forty-two).

"Hey, I got one number this time," Albert said to himself. "I'm getting closer." He laid the ticket next to the first one. "Maybe if I can get a couple more numbers on this last one, I can get a free ticket."

Albert rested the last ticket above the keyboard on his laptop. He took a deep breath and looked at the numbers again.

Five...(five)...Eighteen...(eighteen...again!) ...Twenty-eight...(twenty-eight...woohoo, free ticket)...Thirty-one...(thirty-one)...Thirty-nine...(thirty-nine, gulp)...

Mark was just about to take his shot at the pool table when Albert shrieked like a little girl. He hit the cue ball with so much unintended force that it left the table, went crashing through a plate-glass window and rolled out into the street!

-END-

A Stranger's Whisper

Frank Greene struggled to keep his eyes open. The line in the middle of Old Highway 18 split in two and he wasn't sure if he was still in his own lane. There were no other cars on the road, which was probably a good thing. He closed one eye and the double line became single again. It was 2:00 a.m. and the moonless night was nothing but a blanket of blurry stars. Tall pines on both sides of the road were just black silhouettes that could just as easily have been mountain ranges if one wasn't paying attention. There was nowhere to pull over on the black satin ribbon of highway, so Frank had to soldier on to find a rest stop or gas station. He was so tired.

His '65 Impala rounded a curve and the tires on the right side threw up gravel from the narrow shoulder of the road. A shockwave went through Frank's body causing him to bolt upright and correct his heading. His eyes were wide open for the time being, but he was still exhausted. The road probably stretched out before him, but he couldn't tell for sure because of the darkness. The beams from his headlights converged only a few feet ahead of the car; so that was the extent of his world. That is, except for the vague outlines of the tree line and the stars which seemed to be waiting for him to drift off the road.

The lines began to double again and then fade. Frank's eyes were almost closed when a large rectangle on the side of the road interrupted the wallpaper effect of the tree line. He slowed down and strained to read the antiquated billboard. The sign read LAST CHANCE MOTEL & GAS – 8 MILES. Along the bottom of the sign was the motel's catch phrase...*A Shining Beacon of Hospitality.* The printing on the sign was so faded that Frank had to deduce much of what most of it said. Considering the condition of the billboard, he didn't hold out much hope there would be an actual motel down the road; but it gave him a goal to keep his mind occupied and alert.

He watched the road and his odometer as it ticked off each tenth of a mile. With every passing mile, the number reel seemed to move slower and slower. Frank flicked it with his finger just in case it had stopped working. When it had finally counted down to one mile, he found himself unconsciously holding his breath. He let a long breath out slowly when the odometer finally reached the eight-mile mark. He was getting used to disappointment. Then he saw a brief flicker of neon.

It was only for a second and Frank considered the possibility that it was a fatigue-induced hallucination. He blinked a couple of times and became aware of an outline of a sign and a darkened building. It looked as though no one had stayed at the *Last Chance Motel* for decades. Frank slowed his car and pulled into the overgrown gravel lot to take a closer look and give himself a breather from driving. The weeds growing up through the pebbles muffled the sound of his tires in gravel, so the only sound was the soft rumble of his engine. Frank turned the ignition off and the cooling metal made a plinking sound which seemed to anger the silence. He closed his door softly when he got out, even though there probably wasn't a living human being within fifty miles of the motel.

Frank examined the old sign by using the flashlight app on his cellphone. The words LAST CHANCE MOTEL had been spelled out in neon and outlined in red. The sign boasted of FREE TV and AIR CONDITIONED ROOMS. "Ooooo...*FREE TV*," said Frank under his breath sarcastically. "Such amenities."

The neon words on the sign had painted outlines for greater visibility during the daytime. The sign had been vandalized from individuals driving by. A collection of broken beer bottles lay at the base of the sign post. A few had paper labels that had faded, but were still readable. Frank recognized a few brands no longer in business and wondered how long they had been there. He started to kneel down to get a closer look, but got a mild electrical shock when he touched the signpost. The sign lit up like a…well, a beacon. There was *some* truth in advertising after all. The light almost hurt his eyes as he gazed at the ancient metal sign.

The word *vacancy* and *last* had been completely destroyed by beer bottle projectiles, and the word NO was uncharacteristically bright. The sign now seemed to hold the prophetic warning: *NO CHANCE MOTEL*. Frank removed his hand from the post and the light flickered and went out. Then it came back on briefly with a brighter intensity before going dark once more. The soft buzz of the lights lingered for a moment and then all was silent.

Frank used his flashlight app to continue his exploration of the *shining beacon of hospitality*. An irregular circle of railroad ties that once marked the boundaries of a small playground were decayed and barely evident in the tall grass. The metal frames of swing sets stood rusting in the weeds. The wooden seats of the swings had rotted away, making the rusted chains that hung from the metal frame looked like neglected medieval torture devices. A wooden seesaw had also succumbed to time and weather. It had broken in two and splintered edges rested on the center support. There was a slide that was so rusty, anyone sliding down it would have immediately required a tetanus shot. It must have been a long time since any child had played at the *Last Chance Motel*.

Frank's shadow appeared on the ground before him. He looked back and saw that the sign was lit again. He wondered how it still had electricity running to it. *Surely no one was still paying electric bills on this place*, he thought. He was sure he saw more shadows than his own on the ground, but the light went out before he could investigate further. Turning around suddenly, he caught a glimpse of several silhouettes in his peripheral vision, but there was nothing there but the still night air when he looked directly back. A chill went halfway down his spine before freezing right above the small of his back. It was as if someone had put an ice cube down the back of Frank's shirt. He tried to shake off the feeling of dread he was beginning to experience. He had just about succeeded when he heard a branch break in the woods. Frank stiffened and the jolt actually caused his spine to twist a bit…and he thought he might have peed himself just a little. "Probably a deer in the woods," he said to himself. He wasn't convinced, but he lied to himself anyway.

Frank limped up to the door of the motel office and stood for a moment to keep his knees from buckling. Due to the little spine twist, he had a painful knot where the *ice cube* had been and his left leg was numb. He blamed his injury on the non-orthopedic seats of his 65 Impala and thought it might do for him to get some rest curled up in the back seat in a fetal position. But first, he wanted to investigate the motel office.

There was an old neon OPEN sign in the large picture window that probably hadn't been lit since the Nixon Administration. Tattered sheers covered the window and Frank could only make out a vague outline of the front desk and a couple of chairs. A paper was posted in the window of the door. Time and sunlight had faded it so much that Frank had to move in very closely to examine it.

NOTICE

CLOSED BY ORDER OF TH...

The rest of the page was so faded, it was impossible to read. Frank looked up over the sign. There was a flash of light and a face was looking back at him! His breath caught in his throat as he stepped back, abruptly falling to the ground. He had forgotten about the pain in his lower back, but it all came back to him when he hit the gravel. His back felt like it had been impaled with an iron spike. Seeing the lit reflection of the motel sign in the window of the office, Frank realized it had probably been his own face he saw looking back at him. He began to chuckle uncontrollably and shiver at the same time, which made his back ache even more. *Now I am afraid of my own reflection*, he thought. *Enough investigation. You stopped because you couldn't stay awake. Maybe you should stop playing*

Nancy Drew and get some sleep! Frank could be really hard on himself sometimes, but he knew his inner voice was right. Still, it would be difficult to sleep in a remote location with unidentified noises in the woods and creepy reflections in the windows. It was all too much like the setting of a horror movie.

Frank couldn't shake the nagging feeling that there was something different about the face in the window. The more he thought about it, the less he thought it looked like his own reflection. Instead, it looked a little like someone who was tortured trying to escape. He wondered if the image was something his unconscious mind was generating to illustrate his own feelings of being trapped in a bad relationship. *Well, glad to see those psych classes you took in community college are starting to pay off.* The voice in his head could be a real ass sometimes. Frank cleared his mind and chalked the incident up to fatigue and an overactive imagination.

He struggled to his feet, which *really WAS* torture, and made his way back to his car. He limped and crouched the whole way like a nursing home geriatric. With extreme effort, he strained to take his keys out of his pocket. Wincing with pain, tears formed in his eyes. There was no one around to steal his car, but taking the keys out of the ignition was a force of habit. As he fumbled to find the trunk key on the keyring, Frank paused to collect himself as he opened the trunk. Once the pain had subsided enough, he retrieved an old woolen blanket from under his spare tire. It smelled a little like motor oil, but he crawled into the backseat and curled up under the blanket anyway, using his arm as a pillow. As he lay there, he wished he had started the engine to let the heater run for a few minutes; but he was already settled in and his back had stopped hurting for the time being. He decided to try to make the best of his situation and remain where he was. At least he could finally get some sleep; or so he thought.

Frank's thoughts drifted back to the week before. Caroline had walked in while he was on the phone. Caroline was his fiancée and she thought he was talking to another woman because of his hushed tone. She glared at him and he could feel her gaze on the back of his head. He turned to face her, but finished his conversation. He wasn't cheating on Caroline, but what he was doing was probably just as bad, as far as she was concerned anyway. He was accepting a job offer in spite of her objections. Caroline wanted Frank to work for her father. She wanted to control every aspect of his life. The new job was several hundred miles away and she had no intention of packing up and moving so far from her family. She didn't know that Frank had no intention of taking her. If she had not walked in, she would have found a goodbye note next to the front door explaining his actions and he would have been gone. Sure, it was the coward's way out, but his low self-esteem wouldn't let him stand up to her.

Caroline went through the five stages of grief in less than six minutes, except she skipped right over *Acceptance* and started over again. She paused for a moment on *Denial*, dug her heels in on *Anger* and that is where she remained. Frank finished making his arrangements on the phone and turned just in time to avoid the coffee cup she was hurling toward his head. It hit the wall and shattered like a Christmas ornament and he looked back at her with astonishment. She hadn't intended to miss him. She had thrown the cup with full force and with near deadly accuracy. Only Frank's quick reflexes saved him a trip to the emergency room.

The anger in her eyes was fortified by the twisted curl of the side of her mouth. He stared back at her. Caroline didn't love him. Frank doubted she had ever loved anyone except maybe herself. She had lost control of him and she was willing to go to any lengths to get it back. He felt compelled to argue and then go through his own five stages of surrender. First, there would be *caving in* to her demands; second would be to *apologize* about anything and everything; third would be to *grovel* and beg for forgiveness; fourth would be *self-loathing* for even thinking of opposing her in the first place; and finally, *submission* to all of her demands, no matter how unreasonable. Frank stiffened for the fight which was about to ensue. Then a sudden inner calm washed over him. He looked back at the shattered pieces of the cup on the floor, turned back to Caroline and remarked, "Somebody should probably clean that up." The evil curl left her lips and her eyes widened in disbelief. Frank closed the front door behind him and got into his car. Caroline waited a moment before chasing after him. Screaming like a mad woman from the front porch, most of her words were incoherent and Frank was pretty sure she was frothing at the mouth. That made him shake his head. Fortunately, she didn't use the one weapon against him that he couldn't resist. She never apologized. He knew she never would. Her pride wouldn't let her.

Frank thought it was strange that Caroline had too much pride to say she was sorry or say she was wrong, but not too much to come out in public dressed in a tattered robe and screaming like a mental patient for all the world to see. He didn't wish her any ill will, but he also didn't assist her when she found that she had locked herself out of the house. She would handle it or she would con some unsuspecting soul into helping her. That was how she always handled things. Another fly would be lured into the spider's deceitful web. Frank couldn't help that. He was finally free.

Frank thought he wasn't going to be able to sleep. He was so tired that sleep seemed to elude him. Instead, sleep just came in through a different door. He didn't realize he had been asleep for some time until he heard someone whisper in his ear. At first, he thought it was part of a dream. It was unsettling but not altogether unpleasant. The whisper was so quiet that he wasn't really certain he was awake anyway. He couldn't identify the age or even the gender of the whisperer.

Opening his eyes, he was shocked by a beautiful pair of innocent blue eyes looking back at him. Golden sunlight bounced off the child's face forming an angelic glow. She turned her head to the side and studied him. Frank took a deep breath and could smell honey; or maybe it was clover. It was pleasant, but seemed out of place. Frank didn't question it; he just basked in a fatigue-induced euphoria. He heard another whisper but the child's lips didn't seem to move.

"We are so glad you showed up," said the whisperer.

"I didn't have much of a choice," Frank replied. "I was too tired to go on. I was going to have an accident." The whisperer snickered softly. Then it said, "You are fine now. There is nothing to worry about. Would you like to look around? There is a lot to discuss."

"To tell you the truth," answered Frank, "I would rather stay right here for now."

"Why? You aren't tired anymore and your back no longer hurts. You should come with me."

"I think you are mistaken," said Frank. "I have had this kind of injury before and it doesn't just go away over…uh, how did you do that?" Frank moved around and found his pain to be completely gone.

"Let's go inside," suggested the whisperer. "I have something to show you."

Frank cautiously climbed out of the car and stood up straight. He was careful not to repeat any of the movements which had caused his injury in the first place; but he felt as though he was completely healed. The sun was bright and the trees were vibrant shades of green. There was a glow which was almost otherworldly. The dilapidated playground was new again. A small boy and girl were swinging on the swings and a puppy, probably a beagle, ran under their feet as the children swung back and forth. It yipped as it did and the children giggled.

The blue-eyed child took Frank's hand and led him to the door of the motel office. Another boy slid down the slide as Frank passed. It was shiny and new as well. The boy seemed slightly less cheerful than the children on the swing, but still seemed content. As Frank reached the door, the whisperer said, "It's alright. You will be okay." Frank looked at the child holding his hand. The cherubic face seemed too innocent to be a threat, but he wasn't sure about going into the old motel. Something just wasn't right. He started to turn and felt her grip tighten. "This way," she said. "No need to fear." The whisper was paradoxically calming and disturbing at the same time.

Frank wanted to resist or at least delay going inside, but he found himself standing in the office lobby. He didn't remember opening the door or walking in, which gave him a sick feeling in the pit of his stomach. He was being controlled again and he didn't like it. Neither did he like the room he was in. There was a musty smell of rose petals and talc mixed with an unidentifiable scent. It was by no means pleasant. The combination made him think of rotting meat…at a funeral. The room was bathed in the sunlight streaming in through the sheer curtains which cast everything in a deathly pale.

The lobby looked exactly the way one would expect a motel lobby to look like in the 1950's. There was an overstuffed chair near the front desk and an oxblood colored vinyl couch in front of the window. The couch had chrome plated arms and looked like it would be quite at home in one of your finer bus stations. On the front desk was a vintage bronze lamp with a Tiffany shade. It glowed with a light which seemed to emanate from its base. A vintage television in a light maple cabinet was mounted to the wall.

"You will need a few moments to adjust," offered the whisperer. "Sit down and everything will be made clear soon." The child led Frank to the overstuffed chair near the front desk. He sat down and the soft cushions seemed to caress him. On the table next to him were newspapers dated *1961*. They were small town newspapers and the headlines reported of local child abductions in bold capital letters. Frank spread them out and noticed that their individual dates were only a few weeks apart. Some of the later dates reported multiple abductions on the same day as the unknown subject seemed to grow bolder. He skimmed a couple of the articles, but the headlines seemed to state all of the pertinent information. None of the children had been found and there were no suspects. Once, a delivery vehicle had been spotted near a school, but there were conflicting reports about its description.

The angelic child appeared in front of Frank again and the whisperer said, "I think you are ready now." She placed one delicate finger on the space between his eyebrows. He watched her hand intently until his eyes crossed. He closed his eyes and it felt as though her finger had softly penetrated into his frontal lobe. It made him afraid to open his eyes to make sure it hadn't. He thought the slight but annoying electrical hum was coming from the Tiffany lamp, but he was wrong. It was coming from somewhere deep inside his head. Gray clouds began to form behind his eyelids and he started to get dizzy.

"Just relax," said the whisperer. "Your anxiety will melt away in a moment or two. Let your mind go and I will tell you a story." Frank didn't like to give up control and fought the suggestion. However, the whisper was almost hypnotic and he found himself eager to hear what it had to say.

He finally let go and images began to form. A playground began to materialize before him but it wasn't like the one outside. It was larger, friendlier and more professionally constructed. A city park grew up around it. The trees were full and the leaves reflected a bright summer sun. A soft breeze made them chatter ever so slightly. He could hear the echoing laughter of children, but the playground was empty and the swings hung motionless.

"Why am I seeing this?" asked Frank.

"Wait," said the whisperer. "Focus."

The vision continued. Parked in the street, framed by the posts of the swing set, was a nondescript panel delivery truck that had to be fifty years old or better, but was in perfect condition. It was painted off-white and was unmarked. If it had been any more ordinary it would have been invisible, which was probably the owner's intention. The more Frank concentrated on the truck, the closer he seemed to be to it. He thought he could hear noises coming from inside. They were the muffled sounds of children…and the soft whimpering of a puppy.

"I don't like this," said Frank. "Where is this going?"

"Be strong Frank," the whisperer responded. "This isn't going to be easy for you, but you need to understand."

The panel truck started up and drove out of town. Frank seemed to be following it like a news helicopter. It turned onto Old Highway 18, but the highway didn't seem old. It was in far better condition than when Frank had driven down it just a few hours before. The trip seemed to be happening in *real time* and Frank thought that to be odd. If everything was happening in his mind, he felt it should fast forward over boring details. It seemed to take forever for the panel truck to get to wherever it was going. Frank actually felt as though he was falling asleep inside his own head. He suddenly became aware of the sign on the side of the road.

LAST CHANCE MOTEL & GAS – 8 MILES

A Shining Beacon of Hospitality

The letters were no longer faded and there was a cartoon host on the sign welcoming travelers. Frank couldn't make that line out the last time he read it. Eight miles clicked off much quicker than it did the night before, but it was apparent that the panel truck was on a mission. Still, the driver had kept his speed within the legal limit.

The panel truck turned into the fresh gravel lot of the Last Chance Motel. The metal sign with neon lights looked brand new. So did the small playground. There was a gas pump to the left of the office which Frank hadn't noticed before. The panel truck drove around behind the office and stopped. There were dull thumping noises coming from the back of the panel truck and the sounds of muffled panic. The puppy was whining louder...just short of a mournful howl. A man got out of the driver's side and went over to a double cellar door at the rear of the motel.

Frank wasn't sure he was seeing what he was seeing. The man who got out of the panel truck was very tall and thin. He was bald and had round metal framed glasses; he looked identical to the man in the Grant Wood painting, *American Gothic*. All he was missing was the pitchfork and a plain woman next to him. The man unlocked a comically large padlock and threw both doors wide open. Then he returned to the panel truck, opened the door in the back and gathered up his cargo. The beagle puppy bounded out and ran around the van. It stopped to sniff anything and everything until the man in the glasses gave it a stern look. Then it sheepishly curled up next to the door and was quiet.

Frank watched as the man took two burlap sacks out and threw one over each shoulder. It was obvious from the legs sticking out that one sack contained a boy and the other a girl. The man kicked the panel truck door closed with one foot and disappeared down into the cellar. After a disturbing amount of time, he returned to the truck and retrieved two more bundles of children. This time, both appeared to be boys. They seemed to have resigned themselves to their fates because they weren't kicking.

His final tally was seven in all; four boys and three girls. The man closed the cellar doors and secured the large lock. Then he drove his panel truck further behind the motel and covered it with a large tarp.

Frank felt the small finger being withdrawn from his brain. It made his head swim. He thought that he should be sick to his stomach, but for some reason was not. This bothered him almost as much as what he had witnessed in his mind.

"What was the point of that?" he asked.

"It is important that you know what went on here in the past," replied the whisperer. "You should prepare yourself. It's not the worst thing that you are going to see."

"I don't want to see any more," announced Frank. He was angry at being blindsided by the visions he had already witnessed. They caused suppressed memories of his own childhood to bubble up to the surface.

Frank hadn't been abducted when he was a child, but he had been left in the charge of a trusted family friend for a week when he was six years old.

The family friend's name was Jack. Those first two days had been uneventful...even fun. They played games, went on afternoon excursions and watched cartoons together. Jack had seemed to enjoy the cartoons as much as Frank did. He told Frank that maybe he would take him fishing at the rock quarry the next time he came to visit. Frank had been looking forward to that.

But on Wednesday of that week, things got really ugly. Jack's mood changed and he seemed angry for some reason. Out of the blue, he told Frank that he was not going to get to see his mother again unless he was a *really* good boy. Frank didn't know what he meant by a *really good boy* until Jack pulled him close to him in a rough manner, but kissed him on the head softly. He moved his face in close and Frank could feel his prickly five-o'clock shadow and smelled alcohol on his breath. Jack placed his lips against Frank's and Frank resisted. Jack pushed him to the floor and reminded him of their trip to the quarry earlier in the week and how he had said that *no one would ever find a body thrown in there*. At first, Frank thought he had been joking, but Jack's eyes now showed that he was deadly serious. It was enough to convince Frank to cooperate and keep silent about what happened next.

Frank seemed to have blacked out in his mind, so that those horrific hours of his life were blank; like a missing reel of a movie at the theater. He refused to allow them a place in his consciousness, but their suppression probably led to his succession of bad relationships in his adult life.

"I am sorry about the memories you are having Frank," said the whisperer. "This is necessary. You will see. It is important you know that you are one of us."

"I can't see how," Frank responded. "I think I am still dreaming in the back of my car."

"In a way, you are," said the whisperer. "...but you will need to see more to fully understand."

"I told you, I don't want..." A small finger entered Frank's brain once more and he found himself in a damp cellar ripe with sickening odors. He recognized the smell of mold and mildew, but he feared what the other smells were.

The cellar was larger than Frank thought it should be. It looked as though the motel had been built over the basement of an enormous house. To the right was a coal bin, about three-quarters full. Next to it was a large iron furnace with an unusually large metal door in the front. Orange flames licked menacingly and hungrily through the metal grate in the iron door. On the opposite wall from the furnace was a row of eight tables made out of plywood and two-by-fours. Each table was about five feet long and three feet wide. Many were horribly stained with dried blood. The two tables closest to the stairs were still wet and had what appeared to be lumps of flesh on them. Near the far wall, hooks hung from the joists overhead and shapes hung from the hooks. Frank moved closer to get a better look. Then the scene faded.

"You shouldn't see too much at one time," said the whisperer. Frank was aware that the finger was no longer in his brain.

"Don't you think it is about time you told me what is going on?" asked Frank. "I mean, if this is a dream, it's pretty messed up. I don't know why I would be dreaming it."

"One more place to go and then you will be ready to accept what is happening," answered the whisperer. Each time the small finger touched Frank's head and entered his brain, he felt a little more at peace.

When the next vision appeared, it wasn't disgusting or horrific as he had suspected it would be. It was serene and peaceful. He was in a small clearing in the forest. Wild flowers grew here and there; beams of sunlight filtered through the tall pines. Birds were singing and squirrels were chattering. Frank could make out the *tac-tac-tac* of a woodpecker seeking its next meal.

"Why am I here?" he asked. "I'm all alone here. What am I supposed to see?"

"You're not quite alone," the whisper corrected. "You're in a cemetery."

Frank could make out several irregularly spaced mounds of dirt which seemed to suggest shallow graves. Wild flowers grew on most of them as if they had been intentionally planted there. One longer mound was off by itself. No wild flowers decorated it and grass was loathe to grow on it. Frank was shaken, but regained his composure.

"Is that a grave too?" he asked.

"Yes," the whisperer answered. "Those are the earthly remains of Edgar Chance who built this motel. Over the years, he abducted more than thirty children by using puppies as bait to lure them close to his truck. He managed to avoid detection for a long time. He tortured the children, sexually assaulted them...and mutilated them. When they were no longer useful to him, he dismembered some of them. Others he burned in the furnace. Some he buried while they were still alive. All of their remains are buried here in one condition or another."

Frank felt like he should be emptying the contents of his stomach. The thoughts of such intense and horrible actions were as bad as the Holocaust war crimes he had read about. He didn't get sick, but mentally wretched, which seemed to ease his discomfort a little.

"No one ever suspected him?" he asked after he had recovered.

"No one ever remembered seeing him," replied the whisperer. "He seemed to have a power over people; as if he could make them forget he was ever present. A few children in these graves were snatched from the playground of this very motel. Yet for some reason, no one ever suspected Edgar Chance."

"So what happened to him?" asked Frank.

"People may have been naïve, but not completely blind," responded the whisperer. "A number of years ago, a group of teenagers out for a good time were at the motel when Edgar Chance returned from his latest abduction run. It was probably fate that he hadn't latched the door to the panel truck properly. A child tumbled out wrapped in a sack onto the gravel lot and everyone present saw it. Edgar Chance didn't even try to make an explanation. He just tried to pick the child up and go on about his business. He was that used to getting away with abductions.

"The teens, most of who were on the high school football team, wrestled the child from Edgar Chance's grasp and placed her in the care of their girlfriends. Then they dragged him around to the back of the office. A couple of the more courageous girls found two more children bound in the back of the panel truck. The girls covered the ears of the children, so they couldn't hear the tortured screams coming from behind the motel."

"They killed Edgar Chance?" Frank could not believe that a horrific story like this hadn't made the news.

"They tortured him, they mutilated him...and when they were done with him, they dismembered him. A couple of the teens took his panel truck to the quarry and dumped it in. No one has ever discovered it. No one even questioned his disappearance. It was perhaps ironic that the person who went through life so unnoticed, was also unnoticed when he disappeared. Ironic, but fitting. Edgar Chance was buried in a shallow grave far removed from the rest. I don't think the teens who executed him even knew that they were in the presence of his victims. But we knew," said the whisperer sadly. "...we all knew.

"Those who participated spent the rest of their lives fearing Edgar Chance's shallow grave would be found and that they would be held accountable for their vigilante behavior. The fear was their penance. It wasn't a punishment for them. It was a way of easing their guilt. His grave was never found."

"You were one of Edgar Chance's victims?" asked Frank softly.

"Yes. That's why we're still here," said the whisperer.

"That doesn't seem fair," offered Frank. "You were just kids. Why would you be condemned to such a harsh fate after suffering such torture and horrible deaths?"

"We weren't condemned," responded the whisperer. "This was our choice. Our sacrifice prevents others from sharing our fate."

"I don't understand," said Frank.

"We visit vengeance on Edgar Chance each night in the same ways that he tortured and abused us. We cannot let his spirit rest or it will arise and enter another in the world. The evil which his spirit embodies is very strong and needs to be contained. There are a number like him around the world. When a spirit like his is loosed, terrible things happen. You have seen it on the news. Sometimes, it's a serial murderer who never gets caught. Sometimes it's a tyrant who murders and tortures millions. Others like us around the world confine and torture those individuals when they can. Some of the evil ones have well-known names."

"What a lot to take in," said Frank. "This is a way bigger picture than I could have imagined. They don't teach this stuff in church. It's all kind of new to me."

"There is an old saying; *there's no rest for the wicked.* We make sure that is the case. Were it not for our commitment, we would have moved on long ago. We just can't let it keep happening."

"So you are going to do this forever?" challenged Frank.

"Nothing is forever," claimed the whisperer. "An end will come eventually. We are like soldiers in a war. Either the war will end or our relief will arrive."

"Your relief?" asked Frank. "Someone is coming to relieve you? Who?"

"Someone who shares a little of our history," the whisperer responded. "Someone who can identify with us and believe in our resolve." Frank knew they were talking about him.

"Me? Not me. I've got a lot of things to do," stated Frank. "I am starting a new job on Monday. That's why I was trying to drive straight through the night. I am sorry for what you went through and I really would like to help, but I just can't. I hope you understand."

"We do understand," offered the whisperer. "…but maybe we need to show you one more thing."

"No," exclaimed Frank. "I really don't need to see anything else. I think I have had enough for one night."

"You really need to see this," said the whisperer. A small finger entered Frank's brain and he found himself in the woods once more. This time it was night and there were no small unmarked graves to be seen. He felt himself being drawn toward a glow in a small ravine. There were spotlights at the bottom of it that were aiming at odd angles and at nothing in particular. As he got closer, he realized they were not spotlights; they were headlights. They shined out from each side of a tree trunk that the car had smashed into. A swath of saplings and shrubs had been mowed down behind it from where the car left the road.

A chill when through Frank's soul as he forced himself to examine the driver. He knew what he would find before he got there. The driver hadn't died instantly. The impact of the '65 Impala against the tree had broken the driver's back. His head had smashed against the windshield and the face was unrecognizable, but Frank knew who it was. He didn't know how to react. The five stages of grief probably didn't apply in this situation. The small finger exited his brain and he found himself back in the office of the motel.

"It's really not a terrible fate; not really," suggested the whisperer. "Preventing Edgar Chance from rising is not our sole purpose here. There is much more to it."

"Like what?" Frank asked skeptically.

"Contemplation of our lives," said the whisperer. "Determining what things might have been our fault and determining those times when we were innocent. You can travel back to those times in your past that didn't work out well and change them. You can follow them through and see how they would have worked out in the future. You will acknowledge the wrongs you have done to others and make amends. You will see what you have learned from your mistakes. Mostly, you will spend the time forgiving yourself."

"What difference will it make if it's all an illusion?"

"Life is an illusion, when you think about it," offered the whisperer. "Who's to say what is real?"

"It is not going to be easy to forgive myself if my nights are filled with torturing an old man's spirit to keep him earth bound," noted Frank.

"You should think less about that and more about the countless lives you are saving," the whisperer replied. "It's a job, not a perversion. If torture was something you were going to enjoy for torture's sake, you wouldn't be here. This is karma's way of balancing the scale in your own life. You will be more like a guardian at the gates of Hell."

Frank thought about what she said for a long time. He had not been the best person either and had hurt a lot of people in his life. He thought it might not hurt to score up some points with karma just in case of what might come next.

"I really don't want to do this," said Frank. "...but I have an odd feeling that it is what I am meant to do. Does that seem strange?"

"It's how each of us felt when we first arrived here," said the whisperer. "We didn't want to inflict pain on another human being, no matter what he had done. It wasn't easy at first, but you will see; it gets easier, even gratifying."

"I don't know," worried Frank. "It seems pretty wicked."

"It's not," said the whisperer. "I promise. Come with me."

Frank rose and moved through the door to the motel lot. A host of children awaited him. It was night again and all he could see was their glowing outlines, but he knew they were looking at him with gratitude.

One by one, their glows dissolved into the night until only the one who had taken his hand remained.

"How will I know what to do?" he asked.

"It will come naturally," answered the whisperer. "There is no instruction manual necessary. A few of our number are staying behind to help you. Their journeys are not yet completed."

"I am not sure I am ready for this," Frank said.

"No one ever is; but don't worry," said the whisperer. "You won't have to stay here forever. Someone else will come along."

"In fifty or sixty years?"

"Maybe," said the whisperer. "Maybe tomorrow. Who knows? It depends on when your own journey is over. Someone may come to take your place. Others will most certainly come to help you with your task. It's a new adventure. Embrace it."

With that, the child with the stark blue eyes dissolved into the night. Frank Greene stood in the empty lot and looked out at the dark highway in front of him. This wasn't how he saw the next chapter of his life unfolding. It still felt like his life, even though it was beginning with his death. He dreaded going down into the cellar the way he dreaded going to the dentist for a root canal. He knew it was necessary, but he wasn't in a big hurry to get there.

One of Frank's best traits was that he didn't shy away from his responsibilities, so he forced himself to materialize in the cellar. He thought as long as he needed to get around places, he might as well take advantage of being ethereal. The cellar no longer seemed to be a place of disgust to him. Now it was his workplace for the time being and he needed to get used to that. Edgar Chance lay before him on the table closest to the double cellar doors. He was a naked, rickety old man with his arms and legs bound to the table with copper wire and coat hangers. He looked comic and unthreatening, wearing only work boots and white socks. Three of the older children stood behind him waiting for Frank to join them.

"I am Nate," said the one on the left. "...but you can call me Rusty. This is Jeffrey and this is Abby."

"I am pleased, and at the same time, sorry to meet you," Frank responded. "It saddens me that you had to be here."

"Don't be sad," said Abby. "We are where we are supposed to be for as long as we need to be. It's the order of things. Let's get to work."

Frank thought the kids seemed so much more mature than their appearances would suggest. Then he realized that they had been there for five or six decades. In essence, they were older than he was.

"I'm guessing these bastard kids put you up to this," hissed Edgar Chance. "Well...they won't win. They will never break me and neither will you!"

"From what I have been told," said Frank. "You have always been broken. I'm not here for repairs. I just do maintenance. Let's get started, shall we?"

Edgar Chance was about to fire a volley of obscenities, but Rusty jammed a rolled up pair of socks in his mouth which looked as though they had never seen the inside of a washing machine. Edgar's eyes glowed blue/white with anger and veins stood out on his forehead. There was no torture that could have been worse than the indignation he was suffering at the hands of these children.

Jeffrey produced a rusty butcher's knife and placed its blade against Edgar Chance's chest. "You should watch this closely," he told Frank. He made a deep angled incision from Edgar's collarbone to the bottom of his ribcage. Edgar bit down on the roll of socks while expelling a muffled scream. Frank's eyes widened as he watched the incision expand and white light drifted out of it like glowing vapor. He could make out the features of a child. The child was happy and full of life. Frank breathed in the light and saw the whole life of the child; her joys, her sorrows, her successes and failures. But her life was rich and full.

"That was what you needed to see," said Rusty.

"What *was* that?" asked Frank.

"That was a life saved by our actions here tonight," explained Abby. "When a dark spirit enters the world, countless people are affected. What we do saves more people than you can imagine. That is why it is worth doing."

Frank Greene had always wanted to make a difference. He wanted to be a success at something, but he also wanted to make his mark in the world. He wanted to be remembered. In life, he would hardly be missed. Here, he could make a real difference. *This might not be so bad after all*, he thought.

* * *

Old Highway 18 no longer gets much traffic since the new interstate was completed. People tend to avoid it; mostly because it is so remote. They fear breaking down and not being able to get help. There are also stories about it being haunted. Some people swear that they have heard muffled screams and the laughter of children coming from an old dilapidated motel along the highway. Of course, they never said why they were at the old motel in the first place, so the stories are probably just made up. But the stories about the tortured screams of an old man seem to endure…and the legends become more fantastic with each telling. Legends tend to do that.

-END-

The Pig Man of Heathmoore

The Heathmoore Community School building has sat empty on an isolated county road since its closing in 1974. It was built back in the thirties to accommodate the educational needs of farm families in the area. Safety became an issue in the seventies, so the county decided to use its funds to build two new educational facilities rather than bring Heathmoore up to code. The building was offered up for sale, but no one wanted to pay to have it demolished; and using it for some purpose other than a school was cost prohibitive. Thus, Heathmoore continued to sit empty.

Heathmoore stood as a two-story monument to rural education surrounded by cornfields. A tall brick chimney stood out against a sky that seemed to be perpetually overcast. All of the windows had been boarded up with particle board because every window pane in the structure had been shattered by vandals. The vandalism continued with spray-painted declarations of love... or hate, obscenities and crude depictions of genitalia. The location was too remote for homeless squatters, so the interior of the school remained mostly undamaged except for the broken glass.

An old weathered picket fence surrounding the school property had deteriorated completely in several sections. A rusty metal gate with a decorative metal "H" hung at an angle from a rotting wooden gatepost. The gate moved to and fro in the light breeze; the screech of the timeworn hinges muffled by the wind. The wind itself seemed to be communicating with whomever would listen. Its language was spoken in the form of a whistling moan from the flue of the coal furnace chimney. The agonizing moans kept most people away from this spot; especially in the month of October. The clacking of the dried cornstalks surrounding the school was reminiscent of the sound that wind chimes might make: if the wind chimes were made from human bones. In dim light, the school could easily be mistaken for a haunted mansion, and the screeching rusty hinge underscored the macabre scene.

Boys from the newer high school used the haunted theme to their advantage during the Halloween season. The schoolyard behind the building was a perfect place for them to bring their dates for an evening of romance. The girls were mature enough to know that the stories about the school were made up, but they went along anyway because they too had hormones raging. They just didn't like to show it. Cars would arrive a few at a time, and park in formation as if they were at the Drive-in Theater. Once it was determined that everyone was there, the designated story teller would tell the story of the Pig Man of Heathmoore. This year the designated story teller was a student with the nickname of Crazy Jack.

Crazy Jack would begin by shining a flashlight under his chin to highlight the shadows of his features which were already pretty pronounced. His forehead protruded in Frankenstein fashion. That made his eyes looked exceptionally sunken. He had large teeth and a slight overbite, so in the harsh spotlight his face looked like a skull or death mask. The wind would seem to die down and the chimneys would cease their moaning; almost as if in anticipation of his story.

"It was right here, at this very school, that the Pig Man came into being. He was a student, just like us… except that he was fat… like a pig." Crazy Jack got a chuckle, so he lowered his voice and narrowed his eyes. "They say (pause) he went insane. They say (pause) he couldn't take the teasing and he finally snapped.

"It is said that he lives in this school; down in the boiler room. He feeds off corn and field mice during the summer. But in the fall, when the corn is dry or has been harvested, he has to find something else to butcher and eat. So he waits. He waits until people come around. If a lone car comes down the road and parks behind the school here, well… those in the car may become his meat for the winter. Some say that the boiler room of this school looks like a slaughterhouse with kids just like us, hanging on meat hooks down there. Sometimes, (pause) they are still alive when he hangs them on those hooks. They keep longer that way.

"It's been a long time since anyone disappeared in this area. Pig Man's cupboard is probably getting pretty empty. Soon, he will be looking for fresh meat again, and he will come looking. He will be looking for those who don't think he is real and aren't paying attention. He will come out of the cornfield to take some unsuspecting… GOOD GOD! WHAT'S THAT?!?"

Crazy Jack's eyes widened and he pointed into the cornfield behind the rows of cars. Everyone turned to look. The shadows of the dried cornstalks seemed to dance in the beam of light, eliciting gasps from a few of the teens. The beam of light dropped to the ground and many were sure they had seen the weathered work boots of a maniac. The crowd looked back to Crazy Jack for some sort of reassurance, but he had dissolved into the darkness. Only his still lit flashlight remained, rocking back and forth on the ground. A few of the girls demanded to leave right away. Most of the boys were ready to leave also, but their fear of ridicule by their classmates overpowered their fear of the Pig Man. When Crazy Jack emerged from behind his own car to retrieve his flashlight, he was met with icy stares from half of the crowd and applause from the rest. With the tension broken, the romance went on as usual.

The Pig Man really did exist, but not the way that Crazy Jack described. His real name was Calvin Nettle and he had been a student at Heathmoore a decade or so before. He was very intelligent and he was overweight, but not morbidly so. He lived in a time when obesity was thought to be the result of sloth or gluttony; and the term *eating disorder* was not commonly used. Calvin's eating disorder brought on by emotional distress.

Most of his life, he had been abused by his father in one way or another. His father was cautious enough to make sure he beat Calvin in a way that the marks wouldn't show. He was also emotionally and, some say, sexually abusive to Calvin. He insulted and belittled him every chance he got.

Calvin had also been molested by a neighbor boy and forever carried that secret inside. He shared it only once with someone he thought he could trust. His trust was betrayed by that person. Calvin's self-esteem and reputation were all but shattered. Food and books became his only trusted friends. He ate compulsively while he studied but was determined to escape the small town with small people after high school. He wanted to get as far away from the town…as far away from the other students…and as far away from himself, as possible. He wanted to reinvent himself and never look back.

Unfortunately, Calvin's determination became his downfall. He excelled in every class and that wrecked the grading curve for some of the members of the basketball team. Many had been barely keeping their grades up and two had already been placed on academic probation. In a small school, it wasn't easy for teachers to hide poor academic performance. Midterm tests were coming up and the prospects of a winning year looked dismal. Everyone blamed that on Calvin.

One October evening, three of the team's larger and more dimwitted members drove past Calvin as he was walking on the county road. The weather had turned cold that year and a light dusting of snow was on the dry cornfields. The boy driving the pickup truck skidded to a stop and the other two boys hopped out. They tried to throw Calvin into the bed of the truck but he proved even too heavy for the two of them. The boy driving had to get out and help them lift poor obese Calvin into the truck. They took him to the remote location behind the abandoned school. By the time they arrived, the evening sky was dark and overcast. The boys bound Calvin's hands in front of him with baling wire. It was then that reality dawned on them that they had not thought their abduction through.

"What are we going to do with him now?" said one. "He'll rat us out for sure!"

"I've got an idea," said the driver. He produced a large hunting knife.

"Are you crazy? We can't kill him!" said the third boy.

"We're not going to kill him. We're just going to teach him a lesson."

With that, the boy with the knife proceeded to cut Calvin's clothes off until he was standing in the cold autumn air. He was completely naked except for the baling wire that bound his chubby wrists. Two of the boys laughed and poked his fat sides, but the third felt sorry for him. Calvin's hands had turned purple from the cold and from lack of circulation. His stomach and fat thighs jiggled as he shivered in the cold.

"Now..." said the boy with the knife, "You are going to forget all about tonight, aren't you?" Calvin nodded his head quickly in submission, as he was used to with his father. "...and you are going to start getting a lot of wrong answers on tests; especially the midterms! Do you understand?" Calvin stopped nodding. Books were his friends and his studies were his ticket out of this nightmare he called his life.

"Look," said Calvin. His voice was low and calm. "I really didn't get a good look at any of you. I won't tell anyone what happened here tonight." His voice lowered to almost a whisper. "I would be too ashamed anyway...but I am not throwing the midterms!"

The boy with the knife stopped smiling. He was a respected member of the basketball team and he was not going to stand for any defiance from this naked fat kid. He took another length of baling wire and bound Calvin at the knees.

"Wait here!" said the boy as he dragged Calvin into the cornfield. The other boys tried to protest, but he held up the knife and they stopped talking. They would have left, but the area was so remote and the boy with the knife also had the keys to the truck. Calvin cried and protested as the cornstalks scratched his tender naked skin. The binding on his knees made him walk a little like Mae West in a very tight dress; only clumsy. The two boys left behind were both taking shallow breaths and their hearts were racing. They were sure they were about to become accomplices to murder. Suddenly, Calvin screamed and then began to sob and make gurgling noises. The boy emerged from the cornfield carrying the knife in one hand and something bloody in the other.

"I don't think he will bother us anymore," he said with a sinister tone. He held out his hand to show them the tip of Calvin's nose.

"I suspect he won't return to school after this."

The other two boys began to hyperventilate. One dropped to his knees and had to be helped back to the truck. They drove away slowly; as if they had not just been party to an unspeakable crime. The two boys looked back as they did. They wanted Calvin to be okay, but they really didn't want to see what he now looked like.

Their act of violence proved to be pointless, as they all ended up failing the impending midterms anyway and were suspended from the team.

Calvin had continued to sob and make gurgling sounds as he lay bleeding and nearly frozen between the rows of corn. He had been snorting uncontrollably and was squealing in pain. Knowing he sounded like a pig made him sob and snort even more. It had taken him all night to find his way out of the field and by the time he was discovered, he was suffering from hypothermia. He had irreparable frostbite on his hands and feet due to the cold and lack of circulation to his extremities.

Calvin ended up losing two fingers off of each hand and all of his toes. The muscles in his arms and legs suffered so much nerve damage that the doctors believe they would never fully straighten. They weren't even certain he would ever walk again. Calvin's father didn't even try to show concern for his injured, humiliated and mutilated son. He refused to sign consent forms so that Calvin could be sent to a rehabilitation clinic and treated by a specialist. Instead, he just left the hospital after telling the doctors to do whatever.

He no longer hid his contempt for what was now his hideous son; not that he had been making much of an effort to hide it to begin with. He beat Calvin regularly until finally abuse reports were filed. Calvin was placed in a facility for the disabled as a ward of the state. His mother had died years earlier from "falling down the stairs". Given the violent nature of Calvin's father, it wasn't hard to figure out what had really happened to her. Calvin felt so alone in the world that he wished that he had remained in the cornfield to die of exposure. He really loved his mother and had nothing but hatred for his father; if he really was his father. He had told Calvin on multiple occasions that he wasn't his son; that he didn't know who is father was, but it certainly wasn't him. Calvin knew that his father's denial was his way of coping with the fact that he wasn't a good parent. That still didn't excuse his behavior…or the beatings.

With no one at home to take his aggression out on, Calvin's father began drinking more than usual; which was saying something. He started trying to pick fights at local bars but most of the people played it down. They knew his situation at home and let his behavior slide. Small town folks tend to do that. One night Calvin's father made the mistake of picking a fight with a trucker who was not a regular. The trucker was going through a bitter divorce and didn't back down as the locals did. He took his own aggression out on Calvin's father and left him beaten to a pulp in a ditch about a mile from the bar. When Calvin's father came to, he tried to crawl home but died from internal bleeding and exposure. Karma it seemed, finally got the memo that it was time to make a call.

After several years, Calvin was released from the rehabilitation facility and moved back to the home he had inherited when his father died. A government check provided Calvin with everything he needed. He slept in the master bedroom and he made several trips up and down the stairs each day as a form of physical therapy. Even though he was severely knock-kneed and pigeon-toed (but without toes), he was in pretty good shape. He liked to walk the county roads in the twilight to avoid stares from passersby. Sometimes he would walk all the way to the old Heathmoore School. He avoided it at first because of all the bad memories and destroyed dreams. But his therapist taught him to embrace his past and "own it". Some nights he would leave a little early and risk being spotted on the road. He would hide in the cornfield behind the school and wait for the cars to arrive. Calvin would listen to Crazy Jack and the story that he himself had inspired. Calvin kind of liked being a legend, even an *urban* one. He decided to take an active role in the storytelling. When Crazy Jack got to the part of the story where he said, "GOOD GOD! WHAT'S THAT!?!" Calvin stepped out from the cornfield and squealed loudly. Shrieks came from inside several of the cars. A couple of vehicles made horrible noises from their ignitions being turned over on already running engines. Crazy Jack froze, dropped his flashlight and wet himself. The flashlight fell in such an angle that it spotlighted the dampened crotch of his jeans. He got clipped by another car rapidly leaving the parking lot as he rushed to his own car. Soon, the schoolyard was empty and the only evidence that anyone had been there was a lit flashlight lying in the middle of it. Calvin thought about taking it, but felt it would keep the mystery alive if they returned to find it where it had fallen.

The flashlight was found the next day a couple of the more curious kids who revisited the scene. It was still on but the batteries were nearly drained. Calvin had used an uprooted cornstalk to make something that looked like pig tracks in the soft soil, reinforcing the hoax. It would be some time before the high school boys would brave Heathmoore Community School again with their dates and the legend of the Pig Man of Heathmoore continued to grow. Calvin thought he might reprise his role again someday; maybe he wouldn't. But for now, he had a few more memos to send to Karma.

-END-

Desert Sanctum

Mendel stared into the vastness of space and time and held his breath. He had had no idea that there were so many stars. So many stars filled the expanse, there was hardly any room for darkness. Time and space seemed to surround him. He felt a part of the universe and apart from the universe at the same time. The Milky Way seemed to slash through the very fabric of time and space itself.

Mendel lost himself in the panoramic light show. He lay on his weathered saddle blanket and was absorbed by the moonless desert sky. A few stray meteors streaked across the sky as if to underscore the magnificence of the wonder he was experiencing. By Mendel's reckoning, there was no one within a hundred miles in any direction, so the celestial pageant was just for him. He felt small and insignificant; while at the same time, feeling honored to be witness to it all. Part of him wished he had brought someone along to share it with.

Mendel laid on his back next to the small mound of glowing embers which used to be his campfire. His head rested on his trusty backpack that he had owned since he was a child. Its faded Boy Scouts of America logo was barely visible...even in good light. It wasn't as comfortable as the pillow he had in his jeep, but he wanted to see if he could rough it for a little while. He didn't want to get too comfortable anyway, fearing he would fall asleep and miss all the excitement going on overhead.

He reluctantly got up and added some more kindling and a couple of small logs to the embers. Mendel had bought a bundle of wood at a convenience store when he fueled up his jeep. The wood had been wrapped in plastic and had a convenient cloth strap-handle stapled into one of the logs...just the way the pioneers did it. He burned the stapled log first, along with the plastic. The extra accelerant helped to encourage the fire and he wanted to destroy any evidence that indicated how much of his camping experience was store-bought. The stench from the burning plastic stuck in his nose for a few minutes and it grounded him in reality against his will. Eventually the chemical smell was replaced by the rich scent of mesquite. Mesquite woodchips were something else he had bought at the convenience store. He was pretty sure he wasn't going to find much wood in the desert and he wanted the full survival experience...with amenities, of course.

Mendel had arrived at his chosen destination right around noon, during the hottest part of the day.

He had sat in the shadow of his four-wheel drive, drinking water until after five and waiting for the heat to die down. The heat and the lack of humidity wasn't something Mendel had prepared for. If he had, he would have brought more bottled water. As it was, he would have to leave early the next day. His water supply, while not depleted, would not be sufficient to get him to the next afternoon. There was still water from melting ice in the bottom of his cooler if he needed it, but it wouldn't last long either. Besides, it was gross. Mendel had neglected to clean the cooler the last time he used it.

He chewed on a few ice cubes from the cooler but only a little. The ice served a greater purpose of keeping his bacon and eggs chilled until breakfast. There was also butter and bread in the cooler to make his toast which he was going to prepare *Texas Toast* style by frying it in the large cast iron skillet he brought.

Rocks had been plentiful throughout the area surrounding the campsite and Mendel was proud of the fire pit he had fashioned in the middle of nowhere. He dug out a pit in the sand and placed several roundish rocks in a near-perfect circle around it. On one side, he had placed a single long flat rock which served as a place to rest his cooking utensils and keep his food warm until he was ready to eat it. This proved to be a wasted effort because in the end, he didn't feel like cooking. He fumbled with a manual can-opener (again from the convenience store) and ate pork and beans straight out of the can...cowboy style. While he didn't need the flat stone for keeping his food warm, it was perfect for brewing coffee. He built the fire around five-thirty because he didn't want to go searching for sagebrush kindling after dark in a place known for snakes, scorpions and sand burrs.

The dusk had been breathtaking and left Mendel in awe. He didn't know there were so many shades of oranges, reds and purples. When the sun dropped below the horizon, the colors ran together like jars of paint spilled on a tile floor. They glowed with the light of the now-absent sun in a dreamlike sort of way. The surreal horizon became a black silhouette of buttes, hills and a single Joshua tree which seemed to be lifting its arms in praise of the heavens.

The night sky near the horizon became dark amethyst blending into midnight blue velvet. The sky accessorized itself with a single jewel star. Within seconds, the dark velvet twilight was adorned with stars as plentiful as rhinestones on a singing cowboy's shirt. The light from the stars was so bright, that the silhouette of the horizon remained even after the sun had gone away completely.

Even the best of things can get dull if one gets too much of it. Mendel had taken in the stars for as long as he wanted, but he needed to get about his business of setting up his camp for the night. He unrolled his saddle blanket and placed his backpack at the head of his makeshift bed. Going back to his jeep for a second blanket, he discovered he had failed to bring it. Mendel knew right where it was. He had left it on the foot of his bed at the motel. In his hurry to get to his destination, he had probably left a lot of things back in his room. He hoped it wouldn't get too cold.

Maybe he wouldn't need a second armload of wood, but Mendel mentally kicked himself for not getting one, or maybe two. Six-fifty seemed like a small price to pay now. Mendel went back to his saddle blanket and laid down, propped himself up on his elbow and looked at the fire. A gentle desert breeze blew across the sand and fed the flames. Amber sparks rose up in a futile but earnest attempt to imitate the stars above. As the night closed in around him, Mendel became paranoid about being alone. He kept changing his position around the fire. One reason he moved was because the desert wind was blowing smoke into his eyes. Another was that he had the feeling something was coming toward him from behind. He tried facing the other way, but his imagination saw figures in the darkness.

Mendel tried to ration the logs so they would last the night, but his anxiety forced him to use more than he needed. The fire blazed up with the addition of the new logs and cast a circle of light about fifteen feet in diameter around his campsite. This gave him a sense of security, even if it was false. The flames cast irregular amber patterns in the sand. The images made him uneasy, but at the same time, they mesmerized him. He sat up and stared at them, frozen by their hypnotic dance. The images seemed to come to life and took on three-dimensional aspects. They seemed to be enticing him toward them. The images seemed so desirable; and yet, didn't seem to have his best interest at heart. Mendel had had relationships like that; most of them had been. He knew they were not going to work out and that he should just call it quits, but he always felt powerless to stay away. Mendel usually made bad choices.

The shadows continued to beckon him and he reached out to the images impulsively. A flame leapt up suddenly and jolted Mendel back to reality. He hadn't realized he had begun to move forward and almost placed his hand directly into the fire. He jerked it back and comforted it as though it had been burned. It hadn't, but he took a few moments to be sure. He shook his head and slapped his face as he tried to realign with reality.

His small aluminum pot from Mendel's mess kit was resting on the flat rock of the fire pit. The charred edge of the pot extended over the fire to keeps its contents warm. He picked up the pot, using a rawhide glove as a potholder, and poured steaming coffee into a blue graniteware coffee mug. He was careful to strain out any residual coffee grounds as he poured. Looking at the modest-sized amount of coffee made him wonder how cowboys in the movies always managed to bring a full-sized coffee pot along when all they seemed to have was a pair of saddlebags and a bedroll.

"Hollywood," Mendel murmured. He started when he heard himself break the silence of the night. It was if he had spoken up in church during a silent prayer. There was no one anywhere within miles and yet he was still embarrassed. He sipped his coffee quietly...almost apologetically. He didn't even cry out when he burned his lip on the metal rim of the cup. He did however, make quite a few hand gestures and almost spilled the coffee in his lap. He settled down after a moment and determined he would ignore the injury; even though he was sure a blister had formed. He set the coffee aside and laid back down to once again gaze into the sequined night sky. Before long, he forgot about his burn and was swimming amongst the stars and the earth had ceased to exist.

Earlier in the day, Mendel had driven to the desert from his motel located near Highway 50. He had wanted to get so far away from civilization that it seemed he was on another planet. The spot he found was perfect. It reminded him of Mars. Of course, it also reminded him of westerns from the fifties. The colors had been so brilliant, they shocked his eyes. The mountains in the distance were painted with a purple hue which was impossible for Mendel to describe. One of the main reasons he couldn't describe it was his cell phone didn't get a signal. It really was like he was on another planet. He had tried to send a picture and text his buddy Tim, but he would have to wait until he got within range of a cell tower before he could.

Mendel opened another can of beans. It was fortunate he didn't bring anyone with him. He would not be pleasant company for much of the night; he was sure he would be adding to the planet's methane emissions. He was about to toss the empty can into the darkness, but felt he would be vandalizing the perfect, untouched landscape. He got up from his saddle blanket and placed the can in a plastic bag hanging from the back of his car. The desert gave him a renewed respect for the environment and he paused for a moment to feel guilty about his carbon footprint…and his plastic water bottle. He vowed to do better and went back to the fire. Something made a noise in the darkness and changed his position around the fire once again. Peering into the darkness proved pointless. He couldn't see twenty feet into the blackness. Even worse, he started to imagine the horrible things that might be out there.

Fatigue overtook Mendel. The heat and dehydration had exhausted him and his mind was conflicted. He had so looked forward to escaping civilization, but felt vulnerable now that he was truly alone; possibly for the first time in his life. He thought about his *hunter/gatherer* ancestors and realized why they had travelled in groups. He felt as helpless as a child, but when he returned to tell his tales, he would have braved the wilderness like a mountain man. No one would have to know the truth.

"You could go home now," Mendel said out loud.

"Then they would win," he responded to himself.

"Who are they?"

"Everyone who said I couldn't do it!" he shouted back. His outburst broke a silence that was so pristine, it was as if he threw a brick through a stained-glass window.

"Do what?" His other voice had begun to whisper in mutual respect of the silence.

"Anything...everything," replied Mendel. "My dad was never around; and when he was, he had nothing but criticism for me. He thought his method was good parenting, which probably influenced my choice of friends, because most of them did the same thing."

"Were they jealous of you?"

"You know what? I think they were," he whispered.

"Then why do they matter?" Mendel thought about it for a long time before answering.

"Because they voiced what I feared about myself," he answered softly. "I knew I had flaws and I wanted their acceptance so I could accept myself." A tear formed in the corner of his eye and rolled down the side of his head. It fell into his ear which gave him a chill; he began to shiver uncontrollably.

"Remember what the famous lady said," offered his other voice. "'...no one can make you feel bad about yourself unless you first give them permission.'"

"Maybe..." replied Mendel. "...but there was one thing the famous lady didn't consider."

"What's that?"

"The people we want acceptance from are usually the ones who are the worst about putting us down." Mendel realized he was going in a circle arguing with himself. It wasn't the first time he had had this particular argument, but it seemed to carry more weight in the surreal setting of the desert. Maybe it was the way his words seemed to get lost in the darkness. Or maybe it was the lack of audible distractions. If it wasn't for the mild crackle of the fire or the rustle of sagebrush in the night wind, there would be no noise at all.

Mendel downed what coffee he had left in the cup and pulled the pot back away from the fire as a precaution against burning. He hated the smell of scorched coffee and hated the taste even more. For some reason, it reminded him of tequila. Mendel couldn't stand that either. He laid back down and gazed at the stars once more. He began to breathe deeply, the way he was taught to do in a yoga class he once took. The wind shifted during his second deep breath and he what he breathed in was about fifty percent mesquite smoke. Mendel sat up gasping for air and coughing so violently that some of his coffee returned from his stomach and tried to exit through his nose. It burned his nostrils and made him feel as if he was breathing fire.

After a few minutes, Mendel's coughing spell died down and his nose was almost back to normal. The darkness and silence of the night seemed to be angry with him for causing such a disturbance. Fortunately his fire had burned down and wasn't producing much smoke. The wind seemed to have died down too and the night begrudgingly forgave him for the interruption. Mendel tried to relax again and soon his breathing became regular, but not excessively deep. He stopped focusing his eyes and let his vision direct itself. It was like staring at one of those stereogram posters at the mall. The stars seemed fixed and two-dimensional in his unfocused field of vision. Then suddenly they burst forth and he was surrounded by them. The colors were as brilliant as the desert sunset had been. He felt as though he could touch the stars and he reached out to try. An image appeared in the starry sky like an image on a poster. It wasn't identifiable, but it looked solid and three-dimensional. It had eyes...and teeth. A dragon was staring back at him! Its forked tongue flicked out at him and he stiffened. Then it dissolved back into the jeweled sky.

The stars swarmed around Mendel and he didn't know if he was asleep, awake or somewhere in-between. He felt as though he was swimming in the sky and had lost all sense of connection to the earth. His arms took wide strokes through the heavens and the stars rolled over them in their wake. He flicked his fingers and stars flew away from his fingertips in brilliant streaks. A sense of euphoria overcame him and he was at peace with his inner being. He felt at one with the cosmos. Flashes of light erupted in his peripheral vision and for a moment, he thought a storm might be approaching. Mendel tried to turn his head, but couldn't. He was transfixed by the infinity before him which he now understood. He was at peace with himself and every creature around him; at one with them. He breathed in deeply and became a disembodied entity...floating in a serene ocean of space. The stars winked out one at a time and then in groups. Blackness filled his vision with the exception of a single star directly overhead. It too began to fade and Mendel faded with it.

Time and space ceased to have meaning, so Mendel didn't know how much time had passed before the feeling began to return to his body. He became aware of it without actually waking as he floated effortlessly in the darkness. Moments seemed to expand into years. Slowly, his body started to feel the effects of gravity and the nothingness began to solidify. He became aware of the ground beneath him, his scratchy saddle blanket and the waning heat from his campfire. Mendel also noticed his breathing seemed to be restricted and he felt a strange pressure on his chest. He feared for a moment that he might be suffering from a heart attack. His serenity was gone and panic set in. He opened his eyes and was certain he must still be dreaming. The dragon he had seen in the night sky was staring directly at him. Its angry tongue flicked in his direction and he heard the rustle of its massive scales. Mendel's vision began to dissolve at the edges and he was pretty sure he was about to pass out....if he really was awake.

Mendel felt movement all over his body. His stomach felt like it was rumbling, but not from the inside. Survival mode kicked in and his vision cleared up. His senses became acute. His attention was centered on the rattlesnake coiled on his chest. It rested its huge head on its thick body and kept watch on him. From the ample light of the Milky Way, he could tell there were other snakes on his stomach and a couple on his thighs. Mendel began to perspire out of fear; the rattler's tongue became more active.

"Calm," he told himself. "Be calm."

"You be calm," he whispered back. "What do they want?"

"What do you think they want?"

"I don't want to think about what I think they want," he rasped.

"Your panic is talking now," responded his calmer voice. "What do you know about snakes?"

"They bite people," he answered. "People die. Especially stupid people who are all alone in the middle of the desert when they shouldn't be!" Mendel's voice was louder than it should have been and the snakes slithered and recoiled in an aggravated fashion.

"Those are the things your dad told you to scare you," replied sensible Mendel. "What have you learned about snakes?" Mendel took a slow, deliberate breath and cleared his head.

"Okay," he breathed. "Snakes are cold-blooded. They seek warmth at night. That's why they are on me. They were attracted to my body heat. Some studies show they have infrared sensors of some kind."

"Right," affirmed sensible Mendel. "So they are not here to eat you. They just want to keep warm. What else?"

"The tongue...they smell with their tongues, I think. They smell fear. Oh, crap!"

"So the trick is to not show fear, right?"

"Easy for you to say," said panicky Mendel. "You're not under a pile of snakes."

"Oh yeah...right," remarked sensible Mendel. "If you die, I'll just take the jeep and go home."

"That's not funny," declared panicky Mendel. "What should I do?" The large rattlesnake, disturbed by the conversation, uncoiled a bit and slithered up Mendel's neck and onto his face. It rested its large head directly on his lips. Each time the snake flicked its forked tongue, it went in Mendel's nostril; first one, then the other. Mendel wrinkled his nose and held his breath for as long as he could. *Please don't sneeze*, he thought. *Please God, don't make me sneeze*.

The snakes on Mendel's stomach became agitated by the rattler's movement. They sought to appropriate his spot on Mendel's chest. The rattlesnake withdrew from his face, made a skillfully executed twist, threaded through his own coiled body and faced the encroachers. Poised for striking, he bared his fangs and shook his tail. The sound of the subtle but serious rattle sent a death chill down

Mendel's spine. He was glad he wasn't the recipient of that warning. The others snakes slithered back to their station on his stomach and contented themselves with the body heat they found there.

Mendel began to see white dots in his peripheral vision and realized he wasn't breathing. He feared for a moment he had been bitten when he wasn't paying attention. In reality, he hadn't dare to breathe while the rattler was on his face; however, he had forgotten to start again. He blew a long breath out of the side of his mouth so as not to rile his uninvited guests. He sucked air back in the same way for the same reason.

Laying there wide-eyed and terrified to do anything, Mendel couldn't relax and go to sleep. Even if he could sleep, he feared movements he might make while unconscious would disturb the nest of snakes which had taken up residence on his torso. He was also scared he couldn't stay awake. It had been a long day and the desert night was getting colder. He might start to shiver involuntarily and the result wouldn't be good. The more he thought about it, the colder he got.

Mendel had no idea how late it was or if the dawn would break soon. As a cold sweat broke out on his forehead, he wondered if sweat had a scent, since the rattlesnake who would be king didn't react to it. He was freezing and was sure he was as cold as a corpse. There was no way for him to tell why the snakes had not moved from his cold body and onto the relative warmth of the rocks around his fire. He also had no way of knowing that his campfire had gone out two hours earlier. Even stirring the coals would have done no good. That was the reason the snakes had chosen him as a heat source in the first place.

"Well," Mendel's calmer voice said. "As the *old man* used to say, 'you need to do something; even if it's wrong.'"

"My dad never said that," said freezing Mendel. "You're thinking of some idiot from work. The one who got fired all the time."

"I didn't say which old man." Mendel thought he must be showing signs of hypothermia. If he was suffering from that malady, it meant his body temperature was dropping below 95 degrees. Unfortunately, that was still warm enough to keep the snakes around. If his mental confusion got more serious, there was no telling what he might say or do. He might do something to get himself bitten and then in a confused state, might not be able to drive back to within cellphone range. His fingers were numb and tingly; he flexed them to get his circulation going. A soft rustle of scales and a brief rattle reprimanded Mendel for disturbing his guests.

He wondered just how many snakes were on him. If there were no more than three, he might be able to grab them and throw them into the darkness before they could strike. He discarded that idea almost as quickly as it came to him. Even if he could effectively grab the rattler on his chest, the others were dangerously close to his crotch. Venomous or not, he didn't want any of them biting him down there.

"Maybe if I could throw my voice," he whispered out loud, "I could lead them away."

"You really are confused," said calmer Mendel. "Snakes don't hear like that. Remember? They are more sensitive to vibrations and you're not going to vibrate the air some distance away from your body."

"Why don't you come up with a solution then," asked panicky Mendel. His terror was giving way to anger.

"I already have."

"Would you mind sharing?"

"You're not going to like it."

"I don't have a lot of options right now."

"Okay…but you've been warned." Mendel took a deep breath and waited. The night was deathly quiet. The stars were still just as brilliant, but had lost their luster in his eyes. He waited a full five minutes for an answer before coming to his senses. If he had no answer himself, then no answer would be coming. He knew what his alter ego was saying.

He would have to die. More accurately, he would have to make peace with death. It would give him the edge when he took whatever action he planned to do. He inhaled deeply once more and exhaled through his mouth into the night sky. Then in and out again. Slowly, methodically, he felt like he was becoming one with the earth and sky.

"What a load of crap!" The voice didn't sound like calmer Mendel. It sounded like Mendel's dad. "Just prepare to die already. Forget all the earth and sky stuff. Do you think you're going to do some kind of mystic mind trick on these snakes? They are hardwired to survive. Don't lie to yourself. Accept death."

Mendel didn't want to admit his dad's voice was right. He had been fooling himself into thinking he was doing something heroic, so he still thought he would rescue himself in the end. That wasn't accepting death. He closed his eyes and prepared for what must be the inevitable.

It wasn't really the thought of dying which bothered him. It was the humiliation. There would probably be a news report of an ill-prepared camper, alone in the desert dying of exposure; all because he failed to take proper precautions and bring all the needed supplies. He would be on TV as a cautionary tale to other would-be campers who were considering going into the wilderness alone.

"If you can't be anything else useful in life, you can always serve as a decent bad example."

"Now *that* your dad did say," said calmer Mendel. "Don't worry about the embarrassment. You won't be here anyway."

"You are a regular *Sally Sunshine.*" Mendel was no longer panicky. He closed his eyes, embraced the chill of his body and pretended a coffin lid was closing over him. In his mind, this thought made it easier to accept that he would not see the sunrise. The darkness swirled behind his eyelids and eternity opened out before him. It wasn't bright and shiny with crystal spires and streets of gold. There was no bright light at the end of a tunnel or long-passed relatives waiting to greet him and usher him into an eternal reward. There was only a cold gray darkness…like dirty slush in the winter. It was depressing and unfeeling. There was no euphoria; only melancholy. *Death sucks*, he thought.

"That belongs on a bumper sticker," noted calmer Mendel.

"I didn't think you were coming," said Mendel.

"I kind of have to go where you go."

"Yeah…I guess you do. Sorry."

"They say when you freeze to death, you think you're getting warmer," said calmer Mendel.

"Does it feel like that to you?"

"It kind of does," answered Mendel. "I guess it won't be long now."

He began to feel disembodied, for real this time. He felt as though he was nothing more than his consciousness floating in space. It was a dark, dismal space, but at least he was floating. Mendel felt at peace and was ready to accept whatever eternity had in store for him. Even if it was punishment, he was sure he could handle it. He had prepared for it his whole life. Most of his life was spent in regret of one thing or another. Decisions he had made and the relationships he had formed over the years had been wrong. Regrets had punched holes in the things which had worked out well. He couldn't enjoy them because his past was always right there and he couldn't change it.

"Maybe I don't deserve eternal torment," he reasoned. "...but I don't think I deserve paradise either. Maybe there is something in-between. That would be okay."

A band of light appeared in the distance. It was subtle to begin with, but it was gaining substance with each passing moment. Mendel experienced the warm embrace of compassion and he felt as if a weight had been lifted from him. The light engulfed him and he was ready to be ushered into a life eternal.

"Open your eyes, idiot!" That sounded like Mendel's dad again.

"I honestly didn't expect to see you up here dad," he responded.

"Where the hell do you think you are?" Mendel opened his eyes just a crack and a brilliant light flooded in, causing him to shut them again.

"Earth to Mendel...open your eyes!" He reluctantly obeyed the voice which may or may not have been his own and opened his eyes a little wider. A glowing yellow ball floated above the horizon. Its radiance warmed Mendel's extremities and he shivered uncontrollably. The desert was as beautiful in the morning as it had been at dusk. Sometime before dawn, the snakes had slithered off into the brush to seek rodents for breakfast.

Mendel was still cold, but not frozen as he had thought. He was stiff and his entire body hurt. He made a careful check for fang punctures, especially in his crotch area. Being as cold as he was, Mendel wasn't sure he would have felt it if he had been bitten. He walked stiffly to his jeep to get a plastic bottle of charcoal starter. Placing his last two remaining logs in the fire pit, he doused them with half the bottle of starter. The blaze that rose up was so high Mendel had to back away from it. There must have been at least one live ember in the coals. His hands and feet tingled as blood began to circulate through them again. Mendel didn't like the sensation, but he welcomed it. He was alive after all. He had asked for a place between heaven and hell. And where he was seemed to fit the bill.

The flames settled into a comfortable fire, so Mendel retrieved his bacon and eggs from his cooler. They were still chilled, but all of his ice had melted. He reached in and took a sip of the cooler water from his cupped hand. It tasted like water from a mountain stream. Before long, Mendel had bacon sizzling in the cast iron skillet, and its sharp, savory aroma filled his nostrils. This didn't seem like a point between heaven and hell right now. It seemed a little closer to heaven.

Mendel finished what he believed was the best breakfast and the best cup of coffee he had ever had. He cleaned his cooking utensils *Boy Scout* style...by rubbing them with sand. He was careful to use his rawhide gloves when cleaning them. He might still have to worry about scorpions and sand burrs. It would be a long while before he wished to have another near-death experience.

Mendel probably wouldn't come back to the desert. He was sure it wouldn't be the same. The first time of anything is almost always the best or always the worst. His experience had been both. He wished there had been some way to document it. No one was going to believe it. He packed up his gear and his trash, then aimed his jeep back toward the highway. The warm desert wind blew across his face and he suddenly realized something. He didn't need anyone to believe him. He didn't need to try to impress anyone. If they were his friends, they would take him at his word and be concerned for his safety. If they didn't, they weren't his friends. He didn't need validation from anyone anymore. Mendel finally accepted himself.

-END-

The Darkness Below

Carver Maxwell sat in an upright fetal position in the corner of a seven by seven foot metal box. He had ridden the elevator many times with no incident. Now it was his prison cell. The elevator was descending to the lowest floor of the mortuary when it stopped just two feet above the ground. The lights had flickered a few times before going out completely and the elevator had made a jerky abrupt stop. It was an old model that had been used to move freight. Now it was used to move the recently deceased to the embalming room. It wasn't equipped with emergency lighting, an alarm buzzer or a phone. At the moment, the lifeless elevator was nothing more than a steel cubicle.

Carver tried his best to open the elevator doors, but couldn't get any leverage. He had begun to perspire and the moisture on his hands just made his attempts worse. He reminded himself that the emergency generator would kick in any moment; but filling the generator tank with fuel was one of the items on his to-do list. There had been a rash of outages recently and the generator had been working overtime. Besides, someone would have to reset the breaker before the elevator could function, and Carver was pretty sure no one else was still in the mortuary; no one alive anyway.

The darkness was impermeable and the silence was so deafening that Carver covered his ears to make it stop. Static-like images danced in the darkness. Even closing his eyes didn't help, they were still there. The images transformed into gruesome characters and scenarios of grisly plays written by his unconscious mind. He wasn't sure which was worse; the terrible characters he imagined doing unspeakable things, or the isolating darkness that seemed to be closing in around him. Carver fought hard to forget that a lifeless body lay on the steel gurney next to him in the darkness. It was difficult to ignore because the scent of roses and disinfecting cleaner was stronger than he thought it should be.

Carver's imagination was powerful and a force to be reckoned with. His mind entertained the notion that *he* might be dead, and for some reason that thought was comforting to him. That comfort didn't last long. A low groan came from somewhere and seemed to float in the darkness. Maybe it came from stress on the elevator cables or the emergency elevator brakes. Maybe it came from the body next to him, although he didn't think embalmed bodies made noise. The absolute silence that followed the groan was worse than the noise itself. Carver became aware of another noise. It was a rhythmic clattery sound that seemed to come from everywhere. It took him a moment to realize that it was the sound of his own teeth chattering. He forced himself to get control and took some deep breaths. The smell of roses and disinfectant once again filled his nostrils, making him nauseous. Carver coughed and the sound echoed off the metal walls of the elevator.

The fear of the darkness had driven all rational thoughts from Carver's mind. He could no longer feel anything except the blackness that seemed to have him in a death grip. He never realized before that he was claustrophobic. His fear escalated into panic and taking deep breaths no longer helped. Carver began to convulse and his legs shot out with a nervous reflex reaction. If there had been any doubt, he knew that he was still alive. Dead people didn't have spasms...or did they? Being alive didn't offer him much in the way of reassurance. *Death*, he thought, *I could probably handle. The unknown, not so much.* The elevator shook with his movement and made an echoing thump. He tensed up again and his leg began to cramp. I wonder if this is what rigor mortis feels like when it sets in, he thought. He didn't know technical details of the mortuary business. He had been hired for his muscles; not his brains.

Working at the mortuary had not been Carver's first choice of employment. He didn't own a car and only rode a bicycle to get around. Businesses in town were reluctant to hire him because of that; and because his family had acquired an unsavory reputation. No one talked about it openly when Carver was around, but he heard a lot of whispers and got a lot of sideways glances. He imagined what they were saying behind his back. It couldn't have been worse than what he thought himself, so he never confronted anyone. He just lowered his eyes and moved along.

Carver's younger brother Larry had been killed in a fire. Not just any fire. It was the fire that had destroyed the previous mortuary. The current mortuary had been erected on the same site of it after the foundation and basement had been reinforced. It was the same basement that was just outside the metal box that held Carver captive. No one knew what Larry had been doing in the mortuary in the first place, but it was rumored that he died in the act of committing some kind of deviant sexual perversion. Since no one survived the fire, there was no one who could substantiate the accusations, but rumors carry a lot of weight in a small town.

Carver had a hard time standing up for his little brother because he never trusted him. Larry had always been a bit strange, but more to the point, he was the baby of the family and had been spoiled rotten. It would not have surprised Carver if Larry had engaged in some kind of deviant conduct; but he was family, so he got the benefit of the doubt.

Mr. McNabb hired Carver to assist the maintenance man at the mortuary. He was sure that McNabb had hired him out of pity, but at that point he was willing to take anything. His job encompassed everything the maintenance man didn't want to do or didn't have time for. Carver mowed the lawn, trimmed the hedges and kept the parking lot clear of debris. Passersby found him a little disconcerting because of his appearance. He was tall and thin with long unkempt oily black hair and had a pale complexion. He hardly combed his hair and he was prone to wearing black lipstick to embrace his gothic lifestyle. This visage coupled with his soiled coveralls gave visitors more of an impression of an ax-wielding maniac than that of a groundskeeper.

Lately, many of Carver's duties had been inside. Mr. McNabb thought Carver needed more responsibility to help him raise his self-esteem. He allowed him to assist in the arrangement of flowers around the caskets and viewing rooms. He also charged him with the responsibility of making sure everything was in order before Darrell, the maintenance technician, locked up the mortuary each night. Mr. McNabb always took charge of transporting the bodies himself. A new trend at the mortuary was to have the showing and the funeral on the same day. That way, the bodies didn't need to be returned to the cold room in the basement. Thus Carver had never had to transport any bodies. Due to a last minute request of the family, the schedule changed and that was why Carver came to be in the elevator, alone in the dark with a dead body.

Usually, Carver loved being in the dark silent halls of the mortuary after everyone had left. To him, it felt like being in a horror movie and fit perfectly with his gothic image of himself. His footsteps on the polished marble would echo in the main foyer, and the scuff of his shoes on the carpet would generate thoughts of raspy whispers from beyond the grave. Nearly every night Carver felt the hair on his neck stand up and electric chills run throughout his nervous system; all because he intentionally let his imagination run away with him. He was addicted to the sensation and it never got old. It was ironic that two common tropes of horror movies, thunderstorms and lightning, were things that incited crippling panic in him.

It was that panic he was feeling as he sat huddled, not quite alone in the darkness. On any other night, he would have only been disturbed by his fears, but Carver was terrified of storms and there had been many of them lately, resulting in the power outages that drained the generator. A recent storm had produced such an intense display of lightning that Carver was sure the heavens were after him specifically. His childhood had not been a happy one and he had developed a bit of a persecution complex over the years. The storm that raged outside was about the magnitude of the previous storms that month. He had heard several rumbles of thunder while stacking inventory in one of the upstairs storerooms. He was preparing to finish his work downstairs when another barrage of thunder and lightning hit. Standing frozen in the darkness at the top of the staircase, he could have sworn he saw a wisp of vapor manifest through the main entrance. It was virtually shapeless, but somehow Carver had been sure it was looking up at him from the foyer below. He had remained unable to move until the wisp seemed to move away and drift down one of the corridors. After a few moments had passed, he determined that his imagination was working overtime and cautiously made his way down the stairs. He had stood in the foyer and half-considered following the manifestation down the corridor. While he considered his next action, the foyer filled with a brilliant light as lightning struck close by. Carver had found himself face to face with the most hideous ghoul he could ever have imagined. Thunder erupted and he had let out a higher pitched squeal than he thought possible. Instinctively, he had backed up. The ghoul also retreated. A second, less intense lightning flash revealed the ghoul's true nature; Carver's own reflection looked back at him from a large antique mirror. He uttered a nervous chuckle, but the ghoul still looked disturbing. He noticed that the ghoul had wet his pants but he chose to ignore that. Carver determined that he should probably modify his appearance from then on, and not work so hard at distancing himself from others.

Carver's instructions that evening had been simple, but not very clear. Darrell told him to move the body located in the east viewing room, known as The Manchester, to the cold room for storage overnight. He was then to move the flowers. Carver began to wonder what Darrell actually did. Mostly, it just seemed his job was to tell him what to do. Carver had located a gurney and a clean sheet in the basement, taken it to the Manchester Room. There, he opened both lids of the casket and threw the sheet across it without looking. Dead bodies creeped him out. He had taken a deep breath and lifted the body out of the casket and placed it on the gurney. Moving the body that way hadn't seemed right somehow and felt disrespectful. In the elevator on the way to the basement, Carver began to wonder if Darrell had meant for him to take the casket and all to the cold room. Darrell wasn't very clear with instructions and Carver was a little slow. "Well, it's too late now," he had said to his silent companion.

"Too late now." The voice Carver heard was more of a whisper than an echo. He told himself that it was just his own voice distorted by the metal walls of the freight elevator and the shaft beyond. He tested his theory by loudly pronouncing his own name. The resulting echo did nothing to confirm or disprove his theory.

"C-car...ver!" The strain to keep his teeth from chattering distorted his own name. The voice of the echo sounded less like his own and more like that of his dead brother. It was followed with an unexplained hissing sound. Carver could barely form words but managed, "Is that you Larry?"

"Lar...ry." The distorted response sounded more like a statement than an echo of Carver's question and sounded like it had issued forth from an open grave. Carver tried to position himself as deeply into the corner of the elevator as possible. The echo or the voice, or whatever it was, seemed to be strongest in the front left corner of the elevator.

"Car....ver?" This time he hadn't uttered a word. Larry's voice seemed closer and a little easier to hear; but his sentences were terribly broken and many of his words were garbled.

"Where...*whisper*...body...*whisper*...stolen.
" Carver's mind tried to piece together what Larry was trying to say. Thunder crashed as lightning struck nearby and the walls of the elevator vibrated intensely. Carver thought he could hear Larry clearly when it did. The voice was angry.

"You shouldn't be here," boomed the voice. "You could have stopped me." The voice rumbled like the thunder outside.

"Th-th-there…was nothing I could d-do," stammered Carver. "Y-you wanted that g-girl."

"…that girl," said the voice. "…didn't want me." The voice was a barely audible whisper, if it ever had been real. "…and that girl had a name!"

Carver knew she had a name. It was a name that the whole town knew and a name that had also become part of a scandal. Her name had been Gabriella, but she went by Brie.

Larry Maxwell first saw her at school, but had been too timid to talk to her. When he finally worked up the courage, she shut him down before he could say a word. Her friends had laughed at him as he blushed with shame and he never tried to speak to her again. That didn't stop him from obsessing about her. His obsession was twisted in his mind like a strand of DNA. While he wanted to win her heart, he also wanted to make her pay for humiliating him.

No one knows which of the impulses had driven Larry to hide in the mortuary until the family retired for the evening. He may have only wanted to talk to Brie; or he might have been intending to satisfy his lust for her. Maybe he planned something far more disturbing. It hadn't mattered. Brie wasn't there. As soon as her parents had gone to sleep, she had sneaked out to meet a boy from another school. That thought had probably driven Larry insane; and it wasn't a very long drive to begin with.

The arson investigator determined that the fire that claimed the lives of the Stranton family was deliberately set. The body of Larry Maxwell was also discovered in the ashes of the mortuary. They concluded that he had set the fire but that his motives were unclear.

Brie Stranton had arrived at her home just before dawn to find it engulfed in flames. She had desperately tried to force herself past firefighters to get to her family. She had to be taken to the county hospital to be treated for shock and some second degree burns.

"You couldn't stay out of my business, could you Carver?" The voice spoke with more of a hiss than a whisper.

"Y-you're my brother," said Carver. "I felt like I had to do something. It was her fault you were dead."

"Really?" hissed the voice. "Do you know all the facts; or just what the reports said?"

"I know enough!" Carver's indignation made him a bit bolder. He didn't like being told that he didn't know things. It made him feel stupid. "If she hadn't rejected you, you wouldn't have been there.

The whole thing was her fault. I had to do something."

"You didn't have to anything anymore than I did," hissed the voice. "We are both twisted. You know that, right?"

"I only went to the hospital to tell her off," said Carver. "I wanted her to know what she had done to you."

"But she didn't listen, did she? She just ignored you."

"She just stared straight ahead," said Carver. "She didn't even blink. I thought she was dead, but I could see that she was breathing. It made me mad to be ignored."

"So what did you do," hissed the voice? "You hit her, didn't you?"

Carver began to sob and snort like a toddler. "I didn't think I hit her that hard," he said. "Momma always told us we're not supposed to hit girls. She was just making me so mad!"

"What happened next?" The whisper hissed the question in a way that could only be described as diabolical.

"I don't want to talk about it anymore," sobbed Carver.

"What happened NEXT?" The walls of the elevator reverberated with a loud clap of thunder.

"She fell out of bed," cried Carver. "She hit her head or something! I don't know. I ran out."

"Her brain died, Carver. Her body was still alive, but her brain died. It was your fault."

"I didn't mean for that to happen. It was like she didn't even care what she did to you." Carver's voice bordered on hysterical.

"She finally died you know? Her remaining family pulled the plug so they could donate her organs."

"I-I didn't know that," said Carver softly.

"There are a lot of things you don't seem to know," hissed the voice. "...like who you've been hanging out with."

"What do you m-mean?" Carver's throat was suddenly very dry.

"Did you really think that nothing would ever come from what you did?" The hissing voice that Carver heard was not that of his brother. It was female and it came from right next to him.

"B-Brie S-Stranton? You can't be here!" Carver's voice was only audible to himself, but the voice responded anyway.

"You are the reason I am here," it said. Carver didn't know how to take that sentence. Was she here to exact vengeance on him or was she here because he had technically killed her? In his mind, a wee small voice uttered both!

* * *

Carver Maxwell sat silently in the darkness and wondered how much longer he had to live. He was sure that he had used up all of the oxygen in the elevator and that he would be found dead when he was finally discovered. He thought of how ironic it would be that both he and his brother had both died in a mortuary, and in virtually the same basement. The irony went deeper when he realized that his brother was cremated, while he himself was now entombed. Those were the only two services the mortuary offered. He chuckled again nervously. Brie Stranton would rise from the gurney soon to snuff out his life. He was ready for that now and was sure he deserved it. He let out all the air he had in his lungs and the walls of the elevator absorbed the sound in a morbid way.

Carver resigned himself to his fate and lay on his back with his arms to his sides. His breathing became regular and his muscles relaxed. To his surprise, the static-like images became friendly and inviting. He began to see colors; blue skies, vibrant trees and flowing streams. He looked up at the bright yellow sun. Its glow increased in size until it encompassed the entire sky. Carver began to float up towards the light. This wasn't what he expected. He was sure he should be headed to hell. Instead, he was more at peace than he had ever been in his life. His euphoria was interrupted however, by a force he felt was pulling him back down. It must have been a trick. He was going to hell after all. He felt a heavy "thump" and heard the turning of gears. The doors to the elevator opened and Mr. McNabb stood there looking at him in bewilderment.

"Good God man! Were you asleep?"

"I think I am dead sir," said Carver. Then he realized how ridiculous that sounded. "I mean…"

"Why is Mrs. Coffington on that gurney and not in her casket?" McNabb was certain that he had made a mistake in hiring Carver.

"That's Brie Stranton," said Carver.

"The girl that survived that fire? Are you out of your mind?" Lightning struck outside and the lights flickered again. McNabb's nerves were just about shot. He couldn't help but be just a bit afraid of Carver at the moment. "Brie Stranton isn't dead. Why would you say that?"

"She told me she was…sort of," said Carver. "…anyway, my brother told me she was."

"Your brother…the one that died in the fire? I think we might need to call someone to come get you." McNabb's voice softened and his sympathy for Carver returned. "Let's get Mrs. Coffington into the cold room and we need to get you checked out."

Mr. McNabb would have liked to put Mrs. Coffington back in her casket, but didn't want to trust the elevator any more that evening. The storm had seemed to pass, but he didn't trust the county's electrical grid. He suggested that he and Carver use the stairs instead. They were half way to the first floor when a stray bolt of lightning struck outside and the basement was plunged into darkness. A rasping sound issued from somewhere in the dark and Carver was sure he heard someone whispering. Mr. McNabb heard it too.

-END-

Death Without Parole

The subject of life imprisonment has always been a point of contention in a philosophical sense. The laws are spelled out in detail, but the actual sentence had never been accurately labeled. Was a life sentence designed to be rehabilitation? If so, what was the purpose if there was no chance that the person would ever be released? If parole was involved, then was it really a life sentence? Was a life sentence torture then? To what end? Wasn't torture deemed illegal and immoral?

These were questions that the Honorable Judge Annabeth McIntyre asked herself every time she tried an individual for a capital crime. She poured over many legal tomes trying to find some justification for the sentence; just so she could relieve the guilt she felt with each conviction and sentence. The more she researched and studied, the more she became bogged down in the legalese the system uses to conceal potential mistakes. A loophole of a sort came along with a case of a man being tried for actions so vile that it was a wonder he had survived long enough to even see his day in court.

Maurice "Mo" Zechnich was not a typical serial killer. A serial killer usually stalks his victims as if they were prey. Sometimes, serial killers imprison them for extended periods to make the actual killing more enjoyable. Other times they dispatch their victims right away and then move on to their next quarry. Mo Zechnich abducted, tortured and murdered entire families instead of killing a lone individual. He especially favored large families with several small children. He wasn't a pedophile or a rapist. The torture and anguish on the faces of the parents was what he craved as he tortured their children to death. His soul was a black steaming tar pit which bubbled with hate and rage. If any person deserved torture and a slow agonizing death, it was Maurice Zechnich.

The death penalty was not among the sentences that Judge McIntyre was permitted to pass down. Capital punishment had been abolished in the last general election. Judge McIntyre had no option but to impose multiple life sentences and let some inmate with a homemade weapon finish the job. A job that should have been that of the court. She didn't sleep the night before sentencing.

In one last act of evil, Maurice Zechnich had pled not guilty; even though he was caught in the act of murdering a family of eight. During the trial, he demanded that all of the evidence against him be displayed in the courtroom, even though his attorney advised against it. The prosecution did not object. Crime scene photos were blown up in size and placed on easels in front of the jury. Because of the horrific and graphic nature of the grisly scenes, there were many recesses during the trial. Jurors with weak stomachs had to be excused until they were able to compose themselves. Some witnesses became violently ill on the stand and more recesses were necessary so that the janitorial staff could clean and disinfect.

Some thought the placement of the photos might be a plot by Zechnich to sneak in some accomplice disguised as a janitor to aid in an escape attempt. Before any cleanup could begin, the entire janitorial staff had to be thoroughly searched and their backgrounds checked.

Maurice Zechnich remained stone-faced, but his eyes shined with evil elation. He made no escape attempts. He sat motionless and waited for the proceedings to continue; like a theater patron anticipating the next act of a play.

The prosecution concluded its case on the third day of the trial. As far as they were concerned, it was open and shut. Most of the jury had already made up its mind before the defense even called their first witness. Zechnich's attorney didn't really care. Stanley Nedeljski anticipated that he wasn't going to win the case anyway and had already planned his appeals. Besides, he really didn't like Zechnich and was more than willing to put one in the *loss* column. He informed Zechnich that they would probably lose the case as the judge adjourned the courtroom for the day. Zechnich just looked back at him with a stoic expression that seemed more frightening than a threat would have been. After an uncomfortable moment Zechnich seemed to change the subject.

"Why do people with names that are the most difficult to spell get into the legal profession? Do you just like seeing your name in large letters?" He did something with his mouth that could possibly have been a smile...or a frown; anything really. Stanley Nedeljski began to perspire. He wasn't prepared to defend the spelling of his own name or his career choice.

"I...uh," he stammered.

"I'm kidding," said Zechnich. "I don't have any room to talk. Of course, I didn't become a lawyer. I have my standards." He began to laugh quietly but maniacally; almost as if he was acting. Nedeljski wasn't sure.

"Are you sure you don't have any other witnesses you want to call?" he asked. Stanley was trying to keep Zechnich's sanity in check.

"Just do as I instructed," he said. "Everything will work out."

Stanley Nedeljski was very smart. He didn't go to an Ivy League school, but he had been at the top of his class at the state college. He wasn't just *book smart* either. He could read people, and that was an invaluable asset in the courtroom. He had a pretty good idea what Maurice Zechnich meant by *work out* and the verdict that the jury came back was not going to matter to him. He was already planning to go to prison. Once there, he probably already had an escape plan in the works. A person with a life sentence without a hope of parole has nothing to lose with escape attempts. He doesn't even have to worry about how many people he has to dispatch in the process. Stanley Nedeljski felt dirty in a way that no amount of showering would ever wash away.

Judge Annabeth McIntyre threw up a couple of times in her chambers the morning the defense would present its case. It was important that she got all of the anxiety out of her system; and throwing up seemed to purge her of that. She wanted to present herself in a dignified judicial manner and not look like a Puritan magistrate presiding over a witch trial. Nor did she want to appear weak. She took a Dramamine tablet just to make sure she didn't get sick behind the bench. Judge McIntyre didn't want to give Maurice Zechnich that kind of satisfaction. In her heart, she had already passed sentence on him and felt guilty for that.

The defense didn't bother with character witnesses. There was no one that would testify on Zechnich's behalf and no one would have believed them if there had been. Stanley Nedeljski called only one witness to the stand. It was an expert witness in the field of Criminal Psychology. Dr. Ebbert Patton had been eager to testify, which had initially puzzled Stanley. His motive became clear once he was on the stand. Dr. Patton was not there to bolster a case for an insanity plea. He wanted Maurice Zechnich to be remanded to the Belltower Institute for Behavioral Studies; an institute he himself had founded. He expounded on the benefits that society could glean from studying the psyche of Zechnich and then paused to look each juror in the eye. Somehow he made every one of them feel guilty and uncomfortable. A few thought that maybe *his* psyche should be studied. Others weren't sure it wasn't. Either way, he had made each juror feel as though they themselves were being studied and they couldn't wait for him to get off the stand.

Judge McIntyre clenched her teeth hard because now she had to include Patton's proposal as an option in the deliberation instructions. Since the witness had been called by the defense, she knew it was a ploy by Zechnich to be sent to a facility with minimal security in place. She was planning to send him to a super-max prison, where he would never be a threat to anyone again. Still, she was bound by the law to at least allow the jury to consider the option.

The evidence was piled high against Zechnich and Stanley Nedeljski wondered why he didn't just plead guilty in the first place. It may have been part of a dark plot; or maybe he just like seeing the pictures of his victims again. Zechnich was impossible to read and had very deep pockets. So Nedeljski did what he was told and didn't protest. Zechnich scared him.

The prosecution and the defense presented their closing arguments and the judge gave final instructions to the jury before they were dismissed to deliberate. The testimony of Zechnich's "expert witness" had swayed a few of the jurors and that began to worry the prosecution a bit. Some of the jurors that appeared to be influenced were the more dominant ones who would control the others in the deliberation room. The trial had only taken four days so far but it felt like months to Annabeth McIntyre. Listening to the awful things Maurice Zechnich had done and to see the evidence that was presented had taken so much out of her. It was like a bad dream from which she could not wake up. The irony of that feeling was not lost on her on the day of Maurice Zechnich's sentencing.

The jury had deliberated for nearly three days. Not because some of the jurors thought that Zechnich was innocent. Some wanted him studied for the good of society; the others wanted him locked away for good, also for the good of society. Neither side wanted a hung jury, so eventually those in favor of permanent incarceration caved in. That gave the jury the option of recommending the psychological study and placed the ball of making the final decision firmly in the court of Judge Annabeth McIntyre.

On the day of sentencing, she was approached in the courthouse corridor by a smartly-dressed woman and a man that seemed to be her assistant of some sort. The judge's first thought was to ignore them entirely, just in case they were there on Maurice Zechnich's behalf. Judge McIntyre had agonized over her decision and was ready to hand down her verdict.

"Judge McIntyre. Please, this is very important," said the woman. "I think you will want to hear this." Against her better judgement, Judge McIntyre stopped and turned to address them.

"If you are here about Maurice Zechnich, I cannot discuss his case outside of the courtroom," she said. "The only thing left is the sentencing phase and I have already made my decision."

"I am Dr. Ellyn Abernathy of the Chrysalis Temporal Research Laboratories. This is my associate, Dr. Thomas Islington. If you would just hear us out, I think you will not be sorry that you did."

Judge McIntyre drew a labored breath and replied, "Did you not hear what I just said? I have already weighed the evidence and have made my decision!"

"No doubt you have," affirmed Dr. Islington. "We have been following the case and are fully aware of the sentence that needs to be passed. We are here to offer you a way to fully impose that sentence and satisfy the verdict of the jury without playing into the hands of that monster."

"Thomas…please," said Dr. Abernathy. "I apologize your honor. My associate can be a bit passionate about our research."

"I would be lying if I said I wasn't intrigued," Judge McIntyre said softly. "…but I am also confused."

"Could we speak privately in your chambers?" asked Dr. Abernathy. "I think you will want to hear what we have to present and it would be better if our proposal wasn't made public just yet. It won't take long."

"That sounds suspiciously like something illegal and I don't want any part of it," said the judge.

"There is nothing illegal, I assure you," said Dr. Islington. "Actually there is nothing like this on the books to be illegal. Besides, we aren't trying to influence your decision of your verdict. We just want to give you another choice as to the facility you send Zechnich to."

"How do you know that sending him to a psychiatric facility is the decision I have reached?" Judge McIntyre's still spoke softly, but her tone was stern.

"Our expertise is in the field of Behavioral Studies," said Dr. Islington. "We read expressions, body language...subtle nuances in speech and eye movements. There isn't much that gets by us. We knew the verdict and recommendation that the jury was going to render before they were sent to deliberate."

Judge McIntyre's curiosity went into overdrive but she didn't like being that transparent. Still, she didn't want to have any lingering doubt when she passed sentence, so she invited the doctors into her chambers and hoped she wouldn't regret it. She opened the venetian blinds before sitting down in her large leather-bound chair. The light coming into the dark room radiated around her, creating an aura of authority and control.

"What is your proposal?" she asked. She sat up straight with her hands tightly folded in front of her.

"We know your hands are tied by the law when it comes to imposing the death penalty," began Dr. Islington. "What if we told you that you could impose multiple life sentences though?"

"I can already impose multiple sentences," replied Judge McIntyre. "Have you come here to waste my time?"

"Not at all," said Dr. Abernathy. "What if we told you that you could *enforce* multiple life sentences?"

"Do I have to call security or are you going to leave quietly?" Judge McIntyre picked up the handset of her phone to enforce her threat.

"We are serious," said Dr. Islington. He took a green folder from his attaché case and slid it across her desk. "We are perfecting a program which you might find interesting."

Judge McIntyre looked at the folder suspiciously. It had a symbol on it and the acronym CTRL. She opened it and was relieved to find that the report was written with refreshingly simple terms. Her eyes widened when she came to the content that would apply in her case. The two doctors smiled at each other.

"Let me see if I understand this," she started. "This says that with the application of a panel of drugs, electrical stimulus and sub-sonic sound waves, you can induce a state of consciousness in a person's brain in which an hour would seem like a year. Am I reading that correctly?"

"Essentially yes," said Dr. Abernathy. "…and the possible applications are immense. While under our control, we can manipulate any part of the brain we want. Phobias and mental disorders could be eradicated. College degrees could be obtained in a matter of hours instead of years. Memories of horrific events could be erased, virtually eliminating PTSD and childhood traumas; and we've only scratched the surface."

"I am still not sure what this has to do with me," declared Judge McIntyre. "There must be thousands of volunteers for this type of procedure."

"Volunteers, yes..." agreed Dr. Islington. "Government approval, not so much. Those in office want more trials. They won't sign off on human testing until we have volunteers from the penal system...and only those who are serving life sentences."

"Why life sentences?" asked Judge McIntyre.

"Because part of the agreement is to commute their life sentences," stated Dr. Abernathy. "A reduced sentence acts as a carrot to dangle in front of them to encourage their cooperation."

"Again I have to ask," said the judge. "...aren't convicted criminals lining up for this kind of opportunity?"

"They are," declared Dr. Islington. "...and many have already been selected for the trial."

"Then what is the real reason you are here?" Judge McIntyre folded her arms and sat back in her chair. Tears began to seep from Dr. Abernathy's eyes against her will. She wanted to remain totally professional, but her true agenda was immerging.

"There is a part of this case that was never made public," she responded. "The case you are about to pass sentence on involves me. The family that Maurice Zechnich abducted last was that of my sister and her husband. They were tied to chairs and forced to watch as this monster butchered four of their six children; starting with the youngest. You've seen the crime scene photos. You know how horrible it was and the horror they had to endure. My sister is catatonic and I can only hope that my research can help her. The older children live in constant fear of everything, and never want to leave the house. My brother-in-law has one purpose in life. He wants to make Maurice Zechnich suffer! I can't blame him."

Judge Annabeth McIntyre listened to the story of their grief and despair. She was sympathetic to their plight but was still trying to remain impartial. She had sworn an oath when was appointed judge and had never broken it. Dr. Abernathy was crying openly and Judge McIntyre could tell her tears were genuine. Her own eyes were not succeeding at holding back tears of their own. Dr. Islington, even though he had no connection to the family, was not succeeding at concealing his own grief.

Judge McIntyre thought about her options. Remanding Maurice Zechnich to the CTRL facility would fulfill the intent of the law without sending him where *he* wanted; a place where he probably already had escape measures in place. Additionally, if he was locked in a medically induced catatonic state, he couldn't even make an *attempt* to escape. It seemed too neat; too good to be true.

Dr. Abernathy composed herself a little could before she spoke.

"Honestly, what do *you* think he deserves?" she asked.

"Honestly? He deserves to die...or torture...or both; but only if the law allowed it," answered Judge McIntyre after a very long pause.

"And then what," asked Dr. Abernathy?

"I suppose that is left for God to decide," the judge responded.

"Is it? Really? Do you really think that Maurice Zechnich and his murderous rampages are part of the natural order of things? Is he really part of God's plan?"

"You are getting into an area which is best left to philosophers...not jurisprudence," said the judge.

"Then answer this," said Dr. Abernathy. "What if I told you that we can fix Maurice Zechnich? What if we could make him a productive member of society? What if, by studying him we could prevent other Maurice Zechnichs from murdering more victims? Where do you stand on that?"

Judge McIntyre slid so far down in her chair that she would have slid under her desk had she not stopped herself. It was eight thirty-seven in the morning and she felt like she had done a week's work already. Usually, philosophical questions were discussed in a classroom or at a dinner table. In less than an hour, she could put a philosophical possibility into practice. At the same time, she might be creating a conundrum of her own. She could simply pass sentence with no codicils attached. On the other hand, if she granted the petition of the two doctors sitting here in her chambers, the ramifications could be far-reaching. She might appear weak as a judge and every unscrupulous attorney with a scumbag client would seek to get their case tried in her court.

Dr. Abernathy spoke softly to Judge McIntyre.

"I am sorry to put you in this position," she said. "You have to do what you think is right. You have sentenced a lot of people in the past, I am sure. There were probably some that you wished you could have done more for, but your judicial hands were tied. You now have the chance to literally make the world a better place. The benefits far outweigh the risks. Even if the decision you make today is wrong, it really won't be any worse than questionable decisions you might have made in the past or will make in the future. That is the nature of being human." Dr. Abernathy handed Judge McIntyre another green folder.

"Here are the orders for the procedure," she added. "Everything has been signed and approved. We can complete the procedure by the end of the week. After that, appeals can be granted and your decision can be overturned. Justice can still prevail, but we will have the data we need."

"So does Maurice Zechnich have a say in this decision?"

"Do you really think he would agree to it or deserves one?" asked Dr. Abernathy. "He is psychotic. Think of it as a psychiatric procedure that is being performed in his best interest. I guarantee you; after this procedure he won't even think of appealing your decision."

Judge McIntyre took a deep breath and picked up a pen. She hesitated for a long moment and then signed the order with a slightly shaky hand. "I probably won't sleep well tonight."

"I bet you will," replied Dr. Abernathy. "If not, you will a week from now."

Dr. Abernathy shook Judge McIntyre's hand and looked her directly in the eyes with sincere admiration. Dr. Islington bowed slightly at the waist and the judge thought it was a bit formal for her chambers. After they left, Judge McIntyre buzzed her secretary and gave her the orders to copy and distribute to the officers of the court. She sat in silence for a few moments, contemplating what she had just done. She out a long breath and softly whispered, "What's done is done." That made her feel surprisingly calmer. It was as if a weight had been lifted off of her shoulders. Maurice Zechnich would be someone else's problem now. Maybe he would be the one to have a dream he couldn't wake up from. She prepared to go into the courtroom and pass sentence; but first, she needed to take a Dramamine and go to the bathroom one more time.

How Maurice Zechnich managed to look smug with such a stoic expression was anyone's guess. He was sure he had the judge and the court right where he wanted them. Thanks to the messages his lawyer had sent out for him, he didn't expect to be incarcerated for more than a couple of days before he would disappear and change identities. Then he could get back to pursuing his *passion*.

Everyone rose as the Honorable Judge Annabeth McIntyre entered the courtroom and sat behind the bench. She allowed everyone to be seated and then instructed the defendant to stand.

"Maurice Zechnich. A jury of your peers has found you guilty on four counts of murder in the first degree. In the past, you would have been placed on Death Row to await your execution; but Capital

Punishment has since been abolished. Psychological testing has shown that while you possess and abnormal psyche, you were competent to stand trial. Your own expert witness testified to that.

"Thanks to the testimony of your own Dr. Patton, I have several options available to me to satisfy the verdict of this court. Therefore…it is the judgement of this court that your psychological condition is to be treated at a recognized mental health facility until such time as doctors there determine that you are cured."

Maurice Zechnich's eyes glowed in a way that indicated he was gloating while still showing no visible expression of emotion.

"The officers of the court are instructed to immediately transport Maurice Zechnich to the…Chrysalis Temporal Research Laboratories to serve out his sentence; effective immediately." Judge McIntyre slammed her wooden gavel down and whispered, "…and may you suffer a thousand horrible deaths…without any possibility of parole."

Maurice Zechnich's face showed emotion for the first time since he had been in court. His mouth dropped open and his eyes were glowing coals embedded deep in his furrowed brow. He was about to protest when his lawyer stammered a half-hearted objection. Judge McIntyre entertained it with a simple, *overruled*, and slammed the gavel down again harder. Before Zechnich could protest for himself, he was ushered out of the courtroom, strapped to a gurney and placed in the back of an ambulance.

Stanley Nedeljski rifled through his papers and tried to site legal precedents, all the while muttering, "Belltower...he's supposed to go to Belltower."

"Give it a rest Mr. Nedeljski," said the judge. You can still file your appeal. Relax."

That didn't give Stanley much comfort. He was pretty sure Maurice Zechnich would come after his family now. Stanley didn't want to take his case in the first place, but he was only a junior associate at the law firm and had figuratively drawn the short straw. Eventually, he moved out of the city and got out of criminal law. He became a tax attorney where there was a much smaller chance of receiving death threats.

Judge Annabeth McIntyre thought about leaving the bench; but instead decided the lie in the bed she had made. Sleazy attorneys and lowlifes did populate her court for a while, but not as many as she had expected. Eventually, her courtroom returned to the way it had once been and she thought she did actually detect a drop in serious crimes.

* * *

The Chrysalis Temporal Research Laboratories were located just outside of a rural community, away from any well-populated areas. A long black driveway led back to a nearly empty black parking lot, adjacent to a two-story white building. It looked more like a local clinic than a research facility. The tall cobalt blue windows gave the impression that the building was abandoned.

Maurice Zechnich arrived in a standard ambulance and appeared to have no security detail guarding him. Usually, transporting a prisoner of his notoriety and reputation demanded an armored car and a regiment of armed guards. Maurice Zechnich had been strapped to a stretcher and Emergency Medical Technicians ushered him into the building. There had been an armored vehicle for his transport outside the courthouse, but that had been a decoy to distract reporters, cameras and potential assassins.

The EMTs who rolled Maurice Zechnich into the facilities were actually trained Navy SEALs. Upon entering, they were directed to take him to what looked more like an operating theater than a hospital room. They didn't question it. Their job was to transport and secure the prisoner/patient. Once their assignment was completed, they left as quickly as they had arrived.

Zechnich was secured to an operating table just like the ones in a lethal injection chamber. It made him fear that he had been deceived and an illegal execution was about to take place. He was already studying the leather restraints and possible escape routes when Dr. Abernathy and Dr. Islington came into the operating theater; they stood on each side of him.

"You know you won't be able to keep me here, right?" Maurice Zechnich's voice had a lulling quality to it that Dr. Abernathy found utterly disturbing. "You also know that I am going to skin you alive before I leave. It's just something I have to do. These cuffs won't hold me."

"Well," she responded with a disturbing tone of her own. "...maybe we should just get rid of them then." She touched a display on her tablet and motioned to an attendant to remove the restraints. Zechnich was puzzled, but he wasn't going to give Dr. Abernathy the satisfaction of showing it.

"There," she said. "Is that better?"

"What are you up to?" Zechnich's question was monotone; yet, menacing.

"We don't need these," said Dr. Abernathy. "You're going to be a good boy, right?" She seemed unshaken by Zechnich's tone. One of his eyebrows dropped almost imperceptibly, denoting his mistrust of her.

"So I can move about as I please," he said. In his mind, the statement was a command and not a question.

"Of course," said Dr. Islington. His voice quivered ever so slightly. "Move about as much as you can."

Maurice Zechnich tried to raise his hand. Had he succeeded, he would have ripped out Dr. Islington's larynx, but his arm would not respond to the impulses his brain was sending to it.

"What did you do to me?" Zechnich's monotone was gone and had been replaced with a blend of anger and panic; mostly anger.

"We are regulating what information is being communicated through your central nervous system," answered Dr. Abernathy. "Essentially, we have paralyzed you from the neck down. I suspect, given your personality profile, that the lack of control must be infuriating to you right now." She touched the screen of her tablet again. "If you would like to protest, you may do so now." Maurice Zechnich opened his mouth but could utter no words. His eyes widened as he tried harder to yell and curse, but he could not utter a single sound.

"This will be a one-sided conversation from this point on," said the doctor. "Once our procedure has started, we might need information from you from time to time and we will release your voice long enough to get it. Until then, relax and enjoy the ride."

Dr. Abernathy wanted to laugh but she couldn't bring herself to do it. He wasn't here for her amusement and she wanted to be professional. Showing emotion of any kind would be playing his game. He was there to face justice...or maybe it was revenge. The lines tended to cross in this extreme case.

Maurice Zechnich's eyes were bloodshot from the strain of trying to shoot mental daggers at Dr. Abernathy. She hardly looked up from her tablet as she adjusted settings and made a few calculations. Dr. Islington took a chair behind a large high-definition computer screen and waited. Zechnich's eyes crossed in a comically involuntary fashion before closing. His breathing had been forced to stay steady in spite of his rage. The procedure was initiated and the expression of Zechnich's face softened. Soon, rapid eye movements under his lids were non-existent.

Dr. Islington's screen showed only crude representations of what was going on in Maurice Zechnich's mind, but they were integrated with a series of graphs and 3D models that painted a pretty clear picture of what was going on in his head. Dr. Abernathy had developed an algorithm specifically for him which differed entirely from those that the other test subjects received. Their programs were designed to identify factors in their childhoods that were responsible for psychopathic or sociopathic behavior. Then they could either erase or modify those memories. In essence, the programs were designed to make them new people, better people.

Maurice Zechnich was going to be different. She was not prepared to just let that monster forget what he had done to her family. Fixing him wasn't going to bring those children back and it wasn't going to erase the torture they experienced at his hand. She didn't care what the afterlife was going to hold for this scum. Her plan was to send him to hell in a handbasket of her own making.

Dr. Abernathy had studied Zechnich's case history and marked key events in his lifetime that were likely to have triggered his psychotic mindset. The activity in Zechnich's brain would show them enough to make the adjustments and alterations they needed to make. It was also enough to show them what really got under his skin. A little information can be a dangerous thing in the wrong hands. Dr. Abernathy had made a judgement call as to how to proceed. The orders that Judge McIntyre had signed were intentionally vague on several key procedures. That allowed Dr. Abernathy an immense amount of latitude in Zechnich's treatment. Still, she needed to produce viable results if she was to get the government funding that she wanted.

The technology Dr. Abernathy was using was cutting edge; and implementing it was like being on the razor's edge itself. If she erased the events in Zechnich's life that spawned his behavior, he might not know what he was being punished. She *really* wanted him to know why he was being punished. On the other hand, if she initiated several life sentences, he might go further insane and the punishment wouldn't be effective. Dr. Abernathy had come up with a third option. She smiled at that idea. In truth, that option had been her intention all along.

* * *

Maurice Zechnich's life flashed before his eyes. He didn't feel as though he was dying, but he didn't know for sure how that should feel. He had undergone a couple of near-death experiences in his life, but this wasn't like either of those. This was more like looking through a library's archives as if he was trying to find something specific. His mental review would stop at certain points in his life and become extremely focused. Zechnich would feel a strong emotional surge; usually anger. Then the scene would fade into a bright blank screen and his emotions would continue for a few seconds after. It was like waking from a vivid rage-filled dream, only to discover it wasn't real. He remembered nothing after the scene dissolved, but his anger remained for a long while.

Year after year of Zechnich's life passed in front of his mind's eye in real time. There were many events he didn't remember doing. It was hard to believe he had even been present at them, but there they were. The scenes which played out were not unusual. They could have been events in anyone's life. He hadn't been abused as a child or suffered a tragic loss. He was normal, all things being considered. He was an average student as a child but got no thrill or recognition from those few times he excelled at his studies. He had no desire to make any great accomplishments in academics or sports. Little was expected of him and that was what he gave back. Then one day, he discovered his passion.

Zechnich had been walking home from school and came upon an animal which had been struck by a car. The animal wasn't dead, but was suffering terribly. Zechnich had a hard time identifying what it was because it was covered in so much of its own blood. The animal might have been a large house cat or perhaps a raccoon. It didn't matter. Zechnich had never felt a surge of gratification like he did as he watched that helpless creature suffer. He could have put it out of its misery, but he didn't. He watched it suffer until the moment he saw the life go out of its half-open eyes.

After this experience, Maurice Zechnich made it his life's ambition to enjoy that sensation as much as possible. In his neighborhood, family pets began to disappear. Flyers were tacked to trees and posts on a regular basis. Zechnich smiled with a sense of accomplishment when he read them. He was especially gratified when they offered a reward. It wasn't just having a victim which gave him pleasure; it was controlling the emotions of the families.

His first human victim was a child of five. She was a little girl he snatched from a playground. Her mother had been attending to the girl's two-year-old brother. It only took a moment to drag her into a nearby wooded area. The details which followed that case were horrifying. Many facts were not released to the public because the authorities planned to use them to weed out false confessions; but Zechnich knew those facts and so did the parents of the little girl. He made sure of that with notes and taped messages.

He wanted them to suffer. Not because he had anything against them, but because of the twisted pleasure it gave him to torture the family. The scene began to fade and Zechnich cried out in his mind. He wanted to hold on to that memory.

One by one, the many murders Zechnich had committed passed in front of him like a macabre parade. Each one dissolved into oblivion, no matter how hard he tried to hold onto them. Each murder played out in real time or in slow motion. Time passed in Zechnich's mind slowly so that in an actual twenty-four hour period, twenty-five years passed in his mind. Even though he was physically in his mid-forties, in his dream state he was nearing his seventieth birthday. Then, someone outside his mind hit a replay button and it started all over again. This time, blank spaces appeared during all of those significant points which he had enjoyed so much. He felt rage, but no gratification. He even wondered why he was so angry.

The next time his life replayed, he perceived himself to be a doddering old man of ninety-five. This time, the blank spaces had been replaced with scenes he didn't recognize at first. Zechnich also became aware of a new sensation, and he didn't like it. For the first time in his life, or more accurately *lives*, he was feeling the anxiety and fear of his victims; and feeling it from *their* perspective.

This wasn't how he had imagined they had felt. With all their screaming and crying, he somehow thought they were exhilarated by the terror he inflicted. He actually thought he had been doing them a favor. Now all he wanted to do was to make it stop, but he couldn't. A menacing vague shape would stand in front of him and then he would feel pain; searing pain of a knife wound. Sometimes, the shape would burn him and refuse to stop no matter how much he pleaded. There were always others around him, just out of sight. They represented the family members of each victim. Instead of begging for his release, they laughed at him. He felt as though he was on stage in a crowded auditorium and completely naked. The shame, the rage and the humiliation was unbearable; yet he was force to endure it.

The torture was repeated for each of his victims and Maurice Zechnich came to regret killing so many people. Yet he still didn't feel remorse; only pity for himself.

Someone else was in control of every aspect of his being and he only felt anger and frustration. The scenes were always in a dark room; a room so dark that he couldn't tell if there were even walls around him. A single bright light shined down from above him like an interrogation light. It cast harsh shadows in a circle of light around him.

Zechnich could sense that there was someone or something menacing in the darkness just outside the circle of light. It was something without form, but something that would come for him over and over again through several artificially-induced lifetimes. It was the black steaming tar pit of his own soul and it bubbled with hate and rage. He would be murdered day after cyber day by his own hideous soul until his physical body finally gave out. Thanks to the advances made at CTRL, that wasn't going to be any time soon. He would never be cured; and he would never be released.

* * *

Dr. Ellyn Abernathy filed her report on the test subjects of her experimental procedures. Most of the trials had been complete successes. Those who had been selected to receive academic training had been awarded advanced degrees in less than an afternoon.

One student had to repeat the procedure to acquire the desired result, but it was still a success. Another had no results whatsoever, even with a repeated attempt. There was only one failure in the test group. Maurice Zechnich had lapsed into a coma and was not expected to recover. As a matter of policy, the facility would maintain his life support for as long as necessary at their own expense.

Dr. Abernathy had no intention of releasing Zechnich from his mental prison. Her sister had been in a catatonic state since the attack and was not expected to immerge from it. Her brother-in-law managed to survive with therapy and sedatives. Her oldest niece had tried to commit suicide twice; and her brother, the only other of the siblings to survive, was regularly arrested and sentenced to juvenile detention. Dr. Abernathy would eventually treat their problems, but that would take time. It was one thing to do procedures on a convicted murderer. It was quite another to manipulate the psyches of people you care about.

By the time Dr. Abernathy filed her report, Zechnich was over two-hundred and sixty years old in his mind. Every day in his head was a twenty-five year sentence of darkness and terror he would never wake up from. In two months' time, he would have suffered for a thousand years. Dr. Islington thought there was something biblical about that. He remembered something about Satan being bound for a thousand years. Dr. Abernathy didn't have any regrets about her actions. After all, Zechnich wasn't *physically* suffering. He was just experiencing a very long nightmare.

Maurice Zechnich's mind had become the darkened room. His whole world consisted of the chair he was bound to and the harsh judgmental light shining down on him. The creature in the blackness had devoured all of his memories; both good and bad. He knew nothing else but fear, anxiety and a desire for death that would never come. He thought he might be dead already and this must be his eternal punishment. He was mostly right.

-END-

Extinguished

The rain continued to fall in heavy judgmental drops upon the ground. They slapped the ground with a sound not unlike that of a teacher's ruler smacking against the knuckles of an unruly child. It had been raining all night and would probably continue for the rest of the day. It fell continuously on the back of Clancy Defazio's gray slicker as he prepared to execute his task. The heavy drops pounded his back; almost as if they were trying to get him to reconsider his actions.

There was no thunder or lightning to accompany the downpour. Just rain; lots and lots of rain. There were reports of flooding in some areas, but Clancy had been careful to avoid roads that crossed creeks and streams. He didn't need any added complications to hinder him from completing his task. Many of the back roads had large puddles of water covering them, so he had to be careful not to hydroplane or flood his engine. Driving too slowly would make him look suspicious, but driving too fast would have been risky. Fortunately, there was virtually no traffic on the country roads. Decent people stayed home in weather like this; but Clancy wasn't a decent person. He felt like a monster.

The trees were nearly bare because the heavy rain that had persisted all month had robbed them of their fall colors and foliage. Their nakedness added to the depressing ambience of the gray landscape. Thick clouds completely obscured the sun and Clancy could not even judge what time it was. In his haste he had forgotten to wear his watch; but it really didn't matter. He was going to take however long it took to finish the job. He would have liked to have been better prepared, but it wasn't like he really planned the events that had transpired.

It seemed to take forever to get to his destination and he wasn't quite sure he remembered where it was. It had been a long time since he had been there. With any luck, the gravel road leading back to it would not be flooded. Clancy wasn't counting on being lucky. *Why should luck favor me now? I don't deserve luck.* He was muttering to himself, but his chattering teeth made his words unintelligible. His thoughts were screaming at him loud and clear however.

Clancy had hoped that he hadn't been seen and that, it seemed had fallen in his favor. He almost smiled when he finally found the spot he was looking for. A long gravel access road ran between a cornfield and a sapling-lined fence row. The gravel road made a sharp drop and the water at the lowest point emptied into an almost imperceptible drainage ditch. The ancient cemetery was nearly invisible from all directions and the access road behind it took a sharp turn and dropped down just enough to hide Clancy's car from the main road. On the other side of a wire farm fence was a massive wooded area that would be ideal for his task. He had turned the engine off and sat in the car for a few moments to think things over. It was too late to change his mind anyway. He decided that since he had come this far, he might as well see it through. *In for a penny, in for a pound*, he thought. *Whatever that means.*

Bracing himself for what he was about to do, he pulled his hood up over his head and got out. He had to go back to take the keys out of the ignition so he could open the trunk of his car. As the trunk lid went up, the heavy raindrops beat a ragged rhythm on the vague shape wrapped in a plain gray tarp. It was cumbersome and difficult to lift; even more so when he tried to get it over the fence. Clancy dropped the bundle on the other side and it hit the ground with a loud thud. Clancy felt as though he should apologize to it. A lifeless arm had fallen out of the bundle when it fell, and Clancy stared at it as he followed it over the fence. It looked as though it didn't belong to anything remotely human. Things looked different in the light of day. The stark reality of it all was difficult to process. A chill went down Clancy's spine and was amplified by the cold heavy rain. He was pretty sure he would never get warm again.

Clancy dragged his heavy burden through the trees and got tangled in some sticker bushes. His load seemed to get heavier as he trudged on, as if his own guilt was weighing it down. His rubber overshoes sank into the saturated earth in many places; and at least once the lifeless form dug itself in the soft mud and needed to be extricated. He eventually settled on a spot that was far enough into the wooded area to remain hidden, but not so wooded that the root systems of the trees would give him a problem when he began to dig. Clancy took some time to catch his breath after he laid the tarp bundle down. He could see his breath and wondered just how cold it was. After a few moments he prepared to start digging and then realized he had left the shovel in the car. Cursing and spitting all the way back to the road, he hoped he hadn't locked the keys in the trunk. He hadn't; but he had dropped them at the back of the car where they were almost submerged in a puddle. He wasn't a very good criminal.

Clancy was pretty sure the water had shorted out the battery in his key fob but he could live without that. He cursed some more and then made a final check to see if there was anything else he might have forgotten. He didn't want to make this trip any more times than he had to. Taking some time to catch his breath, he looked out over the small private cemetery and the field of brown cornstalks beyond. The gravestones were ancient and barely legible. Many had been vandalized. They stood like a formal tribunal, condemning his actions and muttering to themselves. The muttering sound was caused by raindrops hitting the dried leaves of the cornstalks, but Clancy felt he was being judged by the spirits of those buried nearby. Part of him wondered how he came to be here and what he could have done differently. A hundred alternative scenarios played out in his mind, but they all ended right back where he was.

Clancy shook violently to snap out of his trance, both mentally and physically. Water droplets flew from his slicker in all directions as if they had been shaken off the back of a wet dog. He needed to get back to the business at hand and the sky was getting brighter. He preferred to do the job while it was still overcast. Bright skies might weaken his already shaky resolve.

Clancy used the shovel to help him over the fence. He was not very tall to begin with and he wasn't in the best physical condition. The first time over had been a strain, and twice he thought his heart might give out. The effort was still pretty taxing, even using the shovel for support. His visible breath seemed to project a foot or so from his mouth. His breathing became much more rapid when he thought that he had lost his way. At one point, he got turned around and found he was headed back toward his car. He took a moment to collect himself and retraced his steps; finally heading back in the right direction.

There was some reassurance to be found in the fact that his trail was so hard to follow. It was almost as if Fate was helping him to conceal his crime. Life however had taught Clancy that Fate often just builds up one's hopes so it can dash them to the ground. He never had a very positive outlook on things.

Clancy stood next to a tree near the spot he prepared to dig into. He tried to imagine what the shallow grave was going to look like, but realized that that was futile in that the whole point was for it to be undetectable. He dug a crude outline of the grave before starting to dig down. Then he looked back at the shape in the tarp and extended the edges back another six inches on each side. He didn't want to have to move the dead weight any more than necessary. The new dimensions looked about right, so he began to dig.

Clancy scooped shovelful after shovelful of muddy earth from the future shallow grave. The ground was so saturated that digging seemed easy, but the hole filled with water after each scoop was removed. He felt like he was making no progress whatsoever and he had to keep stopping to catch his breath. Still, the job had to be done. He tried to remember if there was a rule about how deep one needs to bury a body and recalled it had something to do with the grave needing to be the same depth as the decedent's height. He looked down at the rapidly filling hole and decided that was not going to happen.

There seemed to be a paradox taking place within the grave. The deeper he dug, the more that water seemed to fill the hole. It was like the hole was getting deeper and not getting deeper at the same time. The sky had darkened again and heavier raindrops began to fall. The noise from the rain hitting the dead leaves was nearly deafening. Clancy thought he could hear laughter through the din. It sounded like *her* laughter. That infuriated him and he dug with greater purpose. He hated to be laughed at. Occasionally he looked over his shoulder to make sure she wasn't glaring at him with her mocking expression. It wouldn't have been the first time, but he was going to make certain it would be the last.

The rain began to fall even heavier and the skies again darkened; making visibility an issue. Once when Clancy looked back, he thought the tarp was gone. His heart stopped for a second and he had to move a few steps to see that it was still where he left it. The laughter started again, fueling his rage. His forehead began to literally steam. Clancy continued to dig.

* * *

Clancy Defazio was not a particularly good man, but he wasn't a monster either; at least not before that night. He didn't know what it was that caused him to finally snap. Lord knows he had lots of opportunities to snap before. Maybe it was the combination of alcohol and medication that he shouldn't have taken together. Maybe it was a drop in his blood sugar or a rise in his blood pressure. It was probably a combination of all of those things and a dozen other factors he didn't even know about. Maybe he just finally reached the limit of all he could tolerate. In any case, his wife Relda Defazio knew just how to push his buttons.

Relda was short for Esmeralda; a name she hated. She didn't suffer from bipolar disorder, but she adopted the label just so she could be a bitch to anyone she wanted. Her behavior was an insult to those who actually suffered from bipolar disorder, but she didn't care. The feelings of others were of no concern to her. Clancy came to realize this all too well and all too late. During the early stages of their relationship, Clancy accepted that the problems the two of them had were his fault, even though they often weren't. Relda, seeing that he was willing to take the blame for everything, let him. She even piled on all of the emotional baggage she had accumulated over the years. Clancy always took her insults and criticisms to heart with a bowed head, like a whipped dog. Even on the rare occasions when he did do something right, she could always find fault with it. She would usually dismiss his accomplishments with a smirk out of one side of her mouth and a laugh that can only be described as a contemptuous snort. He grew to hate that snort most of all. It was obvious to outsiders the Relda was projecting her own insecurities onto Clancy, but he couldn't see it. His own insecurity and mired past blinded him to that fact.

Slowly, her abuse approached a tipping point and Clancy began to realize that *everything* could not possibly have been his fault. If it had been, he concluded, why would she have stayed with him? Of course he made excuses for her as he always did. *She was just being nice or she pitied him*; things he knew in his heart were not true; but he stayed with her anyway. She had convinced him –and he had convinced himself- that no one else would have him. He might have been right.

Relda was largely at fault for their problems, both emotional and financial, because of her own twisted psyche. She had an incredibly high opinion of herself and thought she deserved everything she wanted. That attitude was coupled with a massive amount of self-loathing and self-pity. She thought the world revolved around her and that made her paranoid. Relda required constant bolstering of her ego from others while being indifferent to their opinions. She could also choose what her mood was going to be and then change it at the slightest whim.

Clancy was different, but not much better. Deep down he believed he was destined for greatness, but sabotaged any chances at success or happiness that he had. Before he met Relda, his relationships had been staggered and strained. The women he had known could only put up with his self-destructive behavior for so long before leaving him. He had told them lies about his abilities and prospects just to get them into bed. They had even been willing to tolerate his lies, but not the way he let others walk on him and use him. Each time he made up his mind to become a better person, he took the easier path and wound up being the same or worse than before.

Relda made Clancy feel different. She had a way of telling him what he wanted to hear so that he began to feel good about himself. He thought he had finally met *the one* and married her after a brief courtship. That didn't last long though. The honeymoon was over almost before the ink was dry on the marriage certificate. She immediately started belittling him and he immediately fell back into his self-flagellating ways. For Clancy, it was easier to take abuse than to improve who he was. Besides, he didn't want to become a success if he was being shamed into it or if he had to share it with her. That's what he told himself anyway and one reason he never succeeded.

Relda's past was checkered as well. The had a string of lovers –or as she liked to call them, conquests– that extended back to when she was in middle school. Over the years her standards dropped and what they brought to the table was less and less. She would always find another prey before discarding the one she was with. Then, like a spider, she would consume that one until he was nothing but an empty husk. She then simply discarded them like crumpled gum wrappers. But to hear her tell it, they left her without warning or they had cheated on her. Sometimes both. Either way, *they* were always at fault. In a way, Relda and Clancy really were made for each other. At least they took each other off of the market for a while.

Clancy genuinely wanted to fix all his problems; not because he cared, but because he wanted to be the winner. He tried to fix everything, even those things that weren't broken. That drove Relda nuts and she constantly attacked Clancy's failures. She also cheated on him every chance she got and wasn't covert about it. Her lovers weren't always male either. If Relda thought there was anyone she could take advantage of, gender was not an obstacle. She was hoping to find someone who could keep her in the same or better lifestyle than she currently enjoyed. Only then would she kick Clancy to the curb.

Relda had one such prospect on the line, but her mental issues wouldn't allow her to take any direct action that would make Clancy leave her. She had hoped that the clues to her cheating would be enough for him to walk out. Then she could tell everyone that he had left her for no reason and that he had been abusive anyway. Clancy knew in his heart that Relda was cheating on him, but he still felt it was his fault. Besides, he knew what she would tell everyone and he wasn't going to let that go unchecked. His friends tried to tell him that he was being an idiot, but he remained in denial. Eventually everyone stopped having anything to do with him, which was exactly what Relda wanted. She didn't want him to have allies. A prey that is separated from the herd is much easier to subdue.

Relda had not bothered with maintaining her personal appearance since the first year of their marriage. She lived in her own form of denial. When she looked in the mirror, she saw a beauty queen. In reality, she looked like the *before* picture in a fitness ad. Her matted hair stood out from all sides and looked as though a comb or brush could not even begin to tame it. It had once been a vibrant red, but now was the color of dirty sand with streaks of slush-colored gray running through it. She wasn't fat, but she wasn't a beauty queen by any stretch of the imagination. Her scowl was her most unattractive feature and it made it seem as though the rest of her body scowled right along with it. Clancy couldn't explain it; he just grew to hate it.

Clancy had been willing to overlook her imperfections, but that was difficult to do when she would stand in the living room, completely naked, smoking a cigarette and criticizing some fault of his. She thought doing so would be disarming. It was, but not in the way she imagined. She thought she was tempting him with promises of something she wasn't going to let him have. He thought she was behaving like a toddler and that any hope of an intelligent resolution to their differences had vanished. He knew that he wasn't a prize himself and he didn't want to judge; but he wanted the fight to be fair. He thought about taking his own clothes off just to level the playing field, but he didn't want to submit himself to that much ridicule. His physical faults were many and he didn't need to be reminded of them.

Clancy didn't want to be treated that way and he always knew that leaving was an option; but his insecurities made him afraid of an uncertain future. *Better the devil you know than the devil you don't.* He had burned all his bridges and cut all ties with nearly everyone he knew. Early on, Relda had convinced him that she could sue him for everything he had if he left her. Several times he was almost tempted to leave her and see, but voices in his head convinced him to stay. Relda's voice mostly. In his mind, her voice sounded eerily like that of his mother's.

Their last fight had been the same as always, but more intense somehow. Relda had been in the kitchen dressed in a tattered housecoat and an ugly pair of house slippers. Without warning, she began taking dishes out of the cabinet and breaking them. Shattered china littered the floor and sink. She mumbled something about their quality or something and then waited for Clancy to apologize. His only response was a wide-eyed look of shock. She snorted loudly and left the room. When she returned she was completely naked again and started in on him once more. She cut the soles of her feet on the broken shards of cheap china and didn't seem to notice. Clancy knew he was in for a long night.

Relda knew exactly how to push Clancy's buttons and she was like a brat in an elevator, determined that they were going to stop on every emotional floor. She started by attacking his inability to earn enough money to please her; even though his income, while not impressive, was well above the national median. Relda had no more respect for money than she did for people. All of their income, even the money set aside for bills, was disposable income to her. They were always behind with their creditors and the thought of a savings account was nothing but a fantasy. Clancy had tried taking over the household finances a couple of times. When he did, Relda would make withdrawals from the joint account by writing checks out to *cash*. After a few critical checks had bounced, Clancy surrendered his control and turned the financial responsibilities back over to her. Her self-destructive behavior had won again.

Attacking Clancy's role as a provider didn't get the reaction Relda wanted, so she turned to attacking his family. She yelled that it was no wonder he was such a loser because he came from a family of losers; even though her own family was nothing to boast about. Relda went down the list of each of his siblings and noted each of their shortcomings in her eyes. Then she attacked his deceased parents. That got more of a reaction from him and he started to get up. Relda placed her hand on his shoulder and shoved him back down.

"Stay seated little man. You're not going anywhere," she said. "…and you know what I mean by *little man*." She did that smirking snort again. Clancy hated her so much when she belittled him, but so much more so when she snorted. She was smearing blood all over the kitchen tile and he was afraid she was going to slip and fall. He didn't care if she got hurt, but he was afraid he wouldn't be able to keep from laughing. That would be an unforgiveable sin. Clancy wasn't even permitted to roll his eyes at her.

"I don't know why I put up with you," she screamed. Her throat was raspy from years of yelling at him. She stood there naked in the kitchen, waving her cigarette around like a conductor's baton. She used it to emphasize her points and blew smoke directly in Clancy's face. His cough sounded just enough like a chuckle to make her hysterically angry and she launched another volley of verbal abuses. She follow those up with slapping him across the face with her partially closed hand. Her long uneven nails left four parallel slashes that began to bleed. The lines of blood across the wounds looked like wicked notes on a macabre music staff.

Relda saw that her barbs were working so she dug in deeper. "I did you a favor just going out with you the first time. I thought you might have some potential and not be the pitiful loser you appeared to be. Boy, was I wrong. Once a loser, always a loser. If it wasn't for that pittance you call an income and the health insurance, I would have kicked your ass out long ago."

Clancy's forehead felt like it was on fire. He wanted to fight back, but his own insecurity fought against him and he remained seated. Relda knew she had him on the ropes and continued to verbally pummel him. As she did, she had a wicked smile on her lips. Her crooked teeth would show ever so slightly, forming an infuriating sneer. Clancy had dental insurance, but Relda never used it. In her mind, that would be admitting she had a flaw and she wasn't about to do that. It was the same reason she wouldn't go to a mental health counselor for her condition. It was too bad; that might have saved her life.

"You are a worthless piece of shit," she hissed. "…an impotent little nothing that should be put out of its misery. Actually, you should be put out of MY misery!"

Relda's tirade went on for nearly a full hour. She brought up everything Clancy had ever done wrong or hadn't met with her standards. She had a knack for remembering every single one as if it had happened yesterday and would bring them up when he was at his lowest. Then she began to attack each of his body parts individually and how he was never interested in romance with her. After the way she had treated him over the years, he wondered why she would expect him to have the slightest interest in sex; with her anyway. Clancy had never cheated on her, but he had thought about it. After years of abuse, he wasn't sure he would be able to perform, but just the fact that he thought about it made him feel guilty. He sat in the kitchen chair like a suspect undergoing a grueling interrogation.

Clancy felt the anger welling up inside him, but thought it would subside as it always had in the past. Something about this time was different though. His forehead continued to heat up and he could feel his blood pressure rising. The lights seemed to dim and he couldn't really hear over the pounding in his ears. He thought his heart might burst. Clancy didn't remember most of the dressing-down but Relda must have hit on some key trigger words. After the night he had had, they were *hair-trigger* words anyway. Somehow, she found just the wrong button to push.

Clancy didn't have a clue as to how the belt ended up in his hand. He didn't even remember still having it. It was a relic from his hippy days when he wore it with a pair of bellbottoms. The belt was made of thick leather and had a large buckle. It had double metal eyelets all the way around and made a formidable defense weapon back in the day. He was swinging it, almost as if his arm had a will of its own.

The heavy buckle struck Relda in the forehead creating an ugly gash. Blood trickled into her eye, sending her into a rage and gave her a chilling look; like something out of a horror movie. She reached for Clancy's face with her long artificial nails and aimed for his eyes. She had taken nearly everything from him and now she wanted his eyesight too! She was determined to teach him a lesson for even thinking about standing up to her. In a defensive move, Clancy looped the belt around her neck to hold her at bay. She scratched at his forearms and spit a mixture of saliva and blood into his face. Further enraged, he threaded the belt through the buckle with one hand while holding her neck with the other.

Clancy's intention was just to keep Relda under control until she calmed down. Somehow, he knew that wasn't going to happen but he didn't know what else to do. He pulled the belt tight until it crimped her neck. The prongs of the buckle locked into two eyelets and Clancy couldn't get it unbuckled. It was pulled too tight. Relda stopped attacking him and turned her attention to the noose that was now choking her. Clancy tried to loosen it, but she continued to claw at his arms and face. Drops of blood ran down his arms from scratches and dripped onto the carpet. Relda didn't show any signs of fear; only fierce rage. Her bulging bloodshot eyes seemed to be screaming, *how can this worm of a man think he was superior to me in ANY way?* The blood from her forehead completely covered one eye and ran down her cheek like tears. She bared her teeth in a furious yet sardonic way. She would have bitten into Clancy's face if she could have reached him.

Relda dropped to her knees and gripped the belt with both hands. Her face was so purple that she looked comical; like a giant blueberry. Her knuckles were white from holding on to the belt and she fell back onto the floor. She shook her head violently trying to loosen the buckle, but with no luck. She never gave up. Losing was not in her nature. Instead, her time just ran out and she stopped moving.

Lifeless eyes stared at the ceiling and blood ran down the side of her face. Clancy hadn't intended to kill her. He wasn't sure what he had intended to do. He would have saved her if he could, but the buckle wouldn't budge. He reached down to try to loosen it again now that she wasn't struggling against him. As he did, Relda looked directly at him and dug her nails so deep in his arm that he was sure she have severed some nerves. His own rage resurfaced and he stood up, placed his foot on Relda's face and pulled the belt until he heard her neck snap. Her swollen tongue protruded grotesquely through her purple lips; and her face was hardly recognizable as human.

Clancy stared down at her, wondering when he was going to wake up from this awful nightmare. He had become a beast he didn't recognize and that others would not have believed possible. Those that knew Relda though, would not have been too surprised; but the actions of that night were totally out of character for Clancy. It was not in his nature to stand up to anyone. He had been a pushover as a child and grew into a pushover as an adult. Self-loathing was a way of life for him and he wallowed in it. For a moment, as he had been choking the life out of Relda, he had seen his own face in hers. It was as if he was strangling the part of himself that he hated so much. That part had come to dominate him and there wasn't much left after it was gone.

Clancy knew there was no way he was going to get away with what he had just done. It was a crime of passion and even if he only got convicted of manslaughter, there would most certainly be a prison sentence. He wouldn't do well in prison. Convicts sense weakness and that was nearly all he was now. He sat on the sofa and thought for a long time, weighing what few options he had left. In the end, he did what most criminals do; he planned to hide the body.

The expression on Relda's face as Clancy wrapped her in the plastic tarp was an exaggerated version of one he knew all too well. It was a look of degradation and disgust. It was the last time he would have to look at it and he actually smiled for the first time in a long time. Thunder rumbled outside and lightning lit up the night sky. He lifted her lifeless body and noted that she was much heavier than he remembered. Of course, he hadn't carried her since their honeymoon.

Clancy placed her on the ground next to the trunk of his car. He searched for his keys and remembered they were in a bowl next to the door. Leaving her body where it was, he went back in to grab his keys, a gray slicker and overshoes. His mind was racing down a dozen avenues at once, searching for alternatives to his dilemma. It was the first time he ever got rid of a body and he just knew he was going to screw it up somehow. Relda's voice kept telling him that from inside his head.

As he returned to his car, a bolt of panic when through him. The tarp containing the body was gone. He froze and stared at the ground where he had laid her. His eyes refused to believe they were not seeing what they were not seeing. Lightning flashed as the storm approached and the outline of the tarp appeared right where he left it. His mind was playing tricks on him. He opened the trunk and gently laid her inside. He didn't know why he felt he needed to be gentle with her. After everything that had happened, Clancy still couldn't bring himself to be disrespectful. He sat behind the wheel of his car trying to force himself to turn the key in the ignition. His *fight or flight* instinct was telling him to run away, but he knew he couldn't do that.

Clancy thought back to movies he had seen about people committing murder. Sometimes he had thought about how he would have disposed of the body in the story. One thought he had was to bury the body in a cemetery at night. No one would think to look in a cemetery for a dead body. That thought made him chuckle nervously. It was odd and somehow fitting that a cemetery came to mind. He knew of one that was quite secluded with a large wooded area behind it. It was in the country and surrounded by fields that he hoped had not been harvested yet. His hands were shaking as he started the car. He was about to put it in gear when he remembered he needed a shovel. Clancy was never going to get to leave if he kept forgetting things.

The night was mercifully dark as he drove out of his neighborhood. The dawn had broken when he finally found the cemetery, but the skies were still pretty dark. It was like the night was staying around just to help Clancy with his crime. The access road was long and full of water filled potholes, but it was secluded and wasn't flooded. Clancy was grateful for that. He took Relda's body out of the trunk and paused to once again catch his breath.

The woods were overgrown, so Clancy had elected not to carry her. He wouldn't have made it very far if he had. Their combined weight would have made him sink up to his knees in the soft earth. Instead, he had stretched a bungee around her body and pulled her by the belt that was still around her neck. If she had not been dead, she surely would have been after that. She was dead though. Very dead. He had pulled her into the woods as far as he thought safe and then pulled her several yards further. Heavy rain began to fall again as he began to dig. Big droplets of rain.

* * *

It felt like the more Clancy Defazio dug, the less he was accomplishing. The water seemed to be rising as he dug deeper, giving the impression that he wasn't doing anything. With each shovelful of soil he removed, the more mud from the soft sides of the shallow grave would fall in. He was progressing though because he eventually got to a point where he had to stand in the grave to dig any deeper. Because of the water and the sludge, he couldn't tell how deep his legs were buried. He looked over at Relda's body and silently blamed her for what he was having to do.

Clancy decided that the grave was deep enough, or at least as deep as he wanted to make it. He tried to brace himself on the sides muddy sides to get out, but the soft earth gave way each time he did. He laid the shovel across the grave and lifted himself out, surrendering his overshoes to the mud in the process. He cursed Relda again and laid down on the wet ground and felt around for his shoes. They were gone. Most likely, he wasn't looking in the right place. Clancy's blood sugar was crashing and his perception of things was confused. He gave up and went to drag Relda's body to her final resting place in his wet stocking feet. The rain began to fall in torrents and there was a lightning strike nearby as Clancy pulled on the thick belt around Relda's neck. A loud crash of thunder startled him and he fell back on the soggy ground. He was sure he heard her laughing at him as he did.

Clancy picked himself up and clenched his teeth. It was like Relda was still getting the better of him. He had never hated her -or himself- more than at that moment. He continued to pull her to the grave and straddled the hole for one final effort. Relda slid effortlessly into the grave and underneath the water. She sank into the sludge at the bottom of the hole. Clancy smiled at a job well done and stood for a moment catching his breath. As he did, his feet sunk into the ground a bit on each side. Clancy picked up the shovel to support himself. As he did, there was a crack of thunder and the shovel handle cracked with it. Clancy lost his balance and fell forward face down into the shallow grave. The broken shovel fell in after him.

Clancy tried to push up from the bottom, but his arms became mired in the same sludge that had swallowed Relda. The more he struggled, the deeper down he went. He held his breath for as long as he could. As he did, more mud and sludge began to fill the hole. Even if he could have pulled his face from it, there was still two feet of water above him. The mud crept into Clancy's nose and mouth. The more he tried to expel it, the more that seeped in.

Clancy was sure he could hear Relda laughing at him. He knew that laugh all too well. He hated that laugh. *Seriously*, she snorted. *You really can't do anything right! What a total loser!* Clancy managed to grip Relda's legs and pushed himself up. He almost breached the surface of the water when her legs sank deeper in the mud and he lost his grip. The disturbance in the water caused more mud to fall into the grave and sludge covered Clancy's entire head. He heard Relda laughing and snorting uncontrollably as he struggled in his rage. The more he struggled, the deeper down he went.

This was not the way Clancy imagined he would go out. He had thought that one day he might take his own life or that he would die from some wasting disease. He loathed the thought that Relda had won one last time. He couldn't even breathe his last breath. Even that had been taken from him. It was trapped in his lungs by sludge, mud, water and her hateful presence. It was a horrible way to die, but in reality he felt he deserved it. Not because of what he had done to Relda, but for the way he had let himself be treated and the way he had treated himself. Clancy had been his own worst enemy throughout his life. He had been a coward and this was a coward's just reward. He knew that. Clancy stopped struggling and let the sludge fill his throat.

* * *

Mud and water had continued to fill the shallow grave until it no longer existed. After the rain stopped, the mud solidified and the ground became nothing but a flat surface. Leaves fell on top what was no more than a low place in a clearing. Clancy's car was found by a group of teens who promptly vandalized it. It was eventually hauled off to a wrecking yard, parted out and crushed without ever being connected to Clancy Defazio. The Defazio house was never considered to be a crime scene, in spite of the blood and broken dishes. It was however designated a site of a domestic disturbance and two missing person reports were filed. No one knew what happened to the Defazio couple and not that many people really cared. Since their car was also missing, it was speculated that they had fled the state to avoid numerous creditors. The house was repossessed by the bank and the contents were sold at an estate auction to settle unpaid debts.

Whether or not Clancy and Esmeralda Defazio would ever be found remains to be seen. Clancy had extinguished Relda's life and then extinguished his own. Their lives had been like two lit matches, discarded after their fires had gone out. In a way, each of them had died years before. They were just too self-absorbed to know it. As Clancy had said, "Sometimes Fate just builds up one's hopes so it can dash them to the ground." Sometimes even farther down than that. Much farther.

-END-

Entombed

Ramsey stared out of the beveled glass window at the approaching dawn. Another night had passed and as always, he was unable to rest. Some of the clouds had red tints which usually meant rain. Ramsey didn't care. Rain usually depressed him, but depression had become a major element in his daily routine. Ornate wrought iron bars were on the outside of his window, but the bars were not what was holding him prisoner. He really wasn't sure why he couldn't leave; but it wasn't for lack of trying. He placed his hands flat against the glass, but felt nothing. He stopped pounding against the impenetrable barrier long ago. It was frustrating and frustration led to depression. He had had enough of that to last ten lifetimes.

Ramsey Eleanor Coffington had been in banking. That is to say, he owned the bank. In his small town, he also owned the local market, the drugstore, the real estate office and a controlling interest in the local dairy. If it made money, Ramsey had his fingers in it. He had even been in negotiations to purchase the local funeral home. However, the deal fell through when some love-struck pervert of a kid burned the place down with an entire family inside. Ramsey considered this to be a bad omen and had passed on the opportunity to be partners in the construction of a new mortuary. He had always been creeped out by dead people anyway. He would have had to handle the business end from afar, but that just wasn't Ramsey's style.

The rain came as he had predicted and the heavy drops ran down the leaded glass in front of Ramsey's face. To anyone who happened to be on the outside, it would have looked as though Ramsey was crying. But that wouldn't happen for a number of reasons. The main one was that Ramsey didn't cry. He was without feelings and that is what made him so successful in the banking industry. He felt no remorse foreclosing on widows, orphans, single mothers, charities or even family members. It would be an understatement for anyone to say that Ramsey Coffington was heartless. No part of his life gave him joy. He functioned like an organism whose purpose was to relieve a host of dead or dying cells. He felt no sinister pleasure when he did what he did. Neither did he feel regret or remorse. It was a job and was therefore all about the bottom line. The closest he came to a positive feeling was the sense of satisfaction when he went over his accounting records.

Ramsey hadn't always been heartless and unfeeling. When he was younger, he was anything but. As a poet once said, *he gave a girl his heart and she gave it back to him shattered and broken.* He knew the relationship with the girl wasn't real, but he thought it would grow into something genuine in time. It didn't. Instead, she broke up with him at an amusement park two hundred miles away from home, yet still expected them both to have a good time. It was a long day and an even longer and more awkward drive home. Ramsey's heart turned to stone during that drive. In the end, he decided he was better off. Love was expensive and usually disappointing. He had never been disappointed by the acquisition of wealth. The girl who hurt him went on to have three children from three unsuccessful marriages. He often wondered if she ever thought about him and regretted her decision, or at least regretted her timing.

Ramsey eventually did marry, but it wasn't for love. The marriage contract and prenuptial agreements had so many clauses and stipulations in them that they looked like the transcripts from a high profile murder trial. When everything was finalized, Sarah Ivey-Duprés became Sarah Ivey-Duprés-Coffington. She wasn't about to give up either of her hyphenated names, but she wasn't going to minimalize her acquisition of Ramsey either. She wanted everyone to know that she was his partner in matrimony. The whole affair was less like a romance and more like a corporate merger. There was even a section in their marriage contract which laid out every contingency in the event of children coming into the picture. Fortunately, this never happened; some of the conditions were terribly harsh.

The rain began to fall harder. Large drops pelted the window as the wind blew fiercely. Limbs of the tree outside were stripped bare of what few leaves still remained at the end of October. The view from the window began to look like an impressionist painting. Colors ran together and then magically separated as the rainwater drenched the beveled glass pane. Even though his view was obscured, Ramsey continued to look out. There was no music; but in his mind, Chopin's *Nocturne for Piano in C minor* played softly. Rain always reminded him of piano music and the nocturne was just the right amount of depressing. His mind wandered to what his life might have been had he chosen a different path. He wondered how the lives of others might have been different if he hadn't been born. That line of conjecture was a dead end, so he thought of something else...Lionel.

In Ramsey Coffington's life, he had engaged in only a single one-night-stand with a girl who he barely remembered from college. He had been drunk and she had been vulnerable. He left her in the upstairs bedroom of a frat house before dawn. She never even got his real name, but he remembered hers. He would have liked to have said he was sorry for the way he treated her, but it would have required feelings. He had left those at the door when he started college. His goal was to be a success and feelings tended to hinder that goal. *Besides,* he thought, *she will be fine. It was just a college fling. Everyone has those.* However, she wasn't fine.

A few weeks later, she had discovered she was pregnant. She had to quit college because her family disowned her. She took a waitress job and then fell into a succession of abusive relationships. The only good thing to come out of their night together was Lionel. He was named after the fake name Ramsey had given her that night. It was one of the reasons she was never able to look him up. The other reason was that she really didn't want to. She hated him and loved him. His name might as well have been Schrödinger. Of course, Ramsey didn't know anything about having a child until he had been married to Sarah for fourteen years. By then, Lionel was in college himself on a full ride scholarship. Ramsey had looked up Lionel's mother out of curiosity. It amazed him how much information he could obtain through the internet. Some of the gaps still had to be filled in by discretely hiring a private investigator. A secret packet was delivered to Ramsey's office at the bank and he kept it in a private safe deposit box in the vault.

The packet contained pictures and all the background information he needed. Ramsey felt a genuine pang of sadness when he read of the string of hardships Lionel's mother had endured. It further saddened him when he read that cancer had taken her life only seven months earlier. He would have liked to have compensated her for all of her hardships. This was the closest he ever seemed to get to compassion...compensation. When he saw Lionel's picture, it was like looking at a picture of himself in college. The only difference was that Lionel possessed his mother's brown eyes. Ramsey's were blue. He looked up Lionel's age and did the math, even though there was no question in his mind that Lionel was his son. The numbers and dates added up, which was all the banker needed. For the first time in a long time, he had feelings for someone other than himself.

Ramsey thought about setting up a meeting with Lionel, but banished the idea when he thought of the ramifications of word getting back to Sarah. Instead, he set up an anonymous trust in Lionel's name to help get him through the next stage of college or get him started in business if he preferred. His selfless generosity was not without selfish motives; it never was. He didn't want Lionel tracking him down and claiming a portion of his vast estate. That scenario would have cost him dearly and would have been completely unacceptable. Still, he would have liked to have met Lionel, at least once before he died.

The rain stopped, but the sad music continued to play in Ramsey's head. The day was dreary and puddles of water stood everywhere. The wind continued and soon dried the residual moisture on the heavy beveled glass windows. Ramsey had picked those out especially because of their functionality and elegance. There was the slightest green hue to the glass, but one had to look closely to see. The wrought-iron bars were twisted to give them added strength and style. They weren't there to keep Ramsey in; they were there to keep vandals out. So were the heavy bronze doors which had turned green with age. Ramsey looked around at his elegantly appointed crypt and wondered why he was trapped there. It was the largest and most elegant private mausoleum in Asphodel Meadows Memorial Park. Its rose granite walls were tastefully accented with black marble panels on either side of the heavy bronze doors. Above the door, in bas-relief was the name COFFINGTON.

The long, thick beveled glass windows in the doors allowed mourners to peer inside the crypt. Those who were so bold to do so found themselves staring directly at the crypt's main occupant. Not because they could see Ramsey. He was just a spirit and had died years before. It was his likeness they saw. Ramsey Eleanor Coffington's emotionless expression had been permanently captured in a life-sized marble statue which he himself had commissioned. It had been moved to his crypt by the request of Sarah. She thought it was the pinnacle of egotism when Ramsey had it commissioned in the first place; even more so when he petitioned to have it placed in the center of the city park. When he died, she sought to relieve the community of any trace of his arrogance. It was also because she wanted to take center stage in the community and not have to remain in the shadow of her self-centered husband. So the statue was placed into the crypt late in the evening on the same day he was interred in it.

Ramsey couldn't calculate how long he had been dead. It was difficult to count exact sunrises when he was unable to write anything down. Ramsey died on February 4th, 1995. He knew because it was etched in the black marble slab right under his name. All he remembered was that he had been very sick with the flu. When he died, he thought his death was just another hallucination. He had had so many during his illness that it was hard to tell what was real and what was not.

He imagined his funeral and it seemed as if his spirit was wrapped in fog and floated overhead. He looked down at his friends, family and townspeople who came to pay their respects. His black polished casket had silver handles with gold inlays. The casket was closed and he wondered why he would imagine it that way. *Do I just not want to see myself dead?* he thought. *It's not like I was disfigured in some way.* All he knew was that he had trouble breathing. The flu will do that; however, it's not a reason for a closed casket service. He suspected Sarah had something to do with it but he didn't have a clue as to why. Maybe it was cheaper. At least, he could understand that.

Ramsey thought that if his funeral was not a hallucination, he should be able to see the bright light everyone talks about, or family members thronging around him. Nothing like that happened. Instead, he found himself in the middle of the above ground vault he had picked out for his final resting place. There was room for Sarah too, but that was all. He had no intention of sharing eternity with Sarah's next husband...if she had one.

The area inside was a small four by seven foot space with a floor of checked rose and black marble. On each side of the open area were the vaults for the caskets. Each wall was made of rose marble with a black marble slab covering the vault. His name, date of birth and date of death were etched in the black marble and gilded in gold-leaf. In the west wall of the vault was a stained glass window which depicted an image of Saint George slaying a dragon. The glass in the window was comprised mostly of yellows, browns and grays except for a green patch of grass, the dragon's green scales and the crimson pool of blood from the fatal blow of Saint George's lance. The life-sized marble statue of Ramsey portrayed him in a dignified, almost triumphant stance. He had one hand positioned on the lapel of his three-piece suit in the way that triumphant, dignified men often do. He remembered posing for it but he never expected it to end up here. He thought it was supposed to be in the park.

Sarah died a few years after Ramsey did. He was anxious to ask her why his stature had been moved. He remembered watching as her pearl-white casket was placed in the vault across from him. Watching as the hearse pulled away, he wondered if he would see her soon. He never did and always wondered why. He would have liked some company; the whole afterlife thing was confusing to him. Even more so when she didn't show up as a spirit as well. He had so many questions and was confident that she had some of the answers. However, he had even more questions the day Lionel arrived at his tomb.

Had Ramsey thought about it, he would have deduced that Sarah had been given access to his safe deposit box upon his death. She was probably angry that Ramsey had kept the revelation about his son from her; but then realized that, given the nature of their prenuptial agreement, she would have done the same thing. She probably felt sorry for Lionel's mother and considered seeking him out. She didn't though. The estate would be in a state of flux for a while and she didn't need any more complications. Sarah finally did contact Lionel when her health began to fail. When she saw him, it was like looking at the Ramsey she had married. At first, she thought she was hallucinating and that her life was over. It nearly was, but he wasn't a hallucination. Lionel was a gentleman, but not particularly compassionate. He and his mother had lived through some hard times and his mother died well before her time.

Sarah amended her own will to give Lionel a substantial portion of the estate. She wasn't going to need it where she was going and there were no other relatives close to bequeath it to. A few charities received generous donations, but the bulk of her estate went to Lionel. She left instructions that he could legally take his father's last name if he wanted to; he passed on that. He took the inheritance even though he wasn't in dire need of finances. He had become successful on his own without help from anyone, which was the way he preferred it. However, Lionel did feel he was owed something, at least for his mother's sake. He also had a wife and two small boys...grandchildren Ramsey would never know.

Lionel did visit the tomb once. He had a volume of things he wanted to say. He stood silently for a few moments facing the bronze doors while Ramsey waited to hear them. Then Lionel just walked away without saying a word. He went on to start several charities in his mother's name; especially one for cancer research. But Lionel never mentioned Ramsey's name for the rest of his own life.

As the years passed, Ramsey looked out over the tombstones from his marble prison. Being a spirit, he thought he should just be able to go right through the wall and move on to the next level of existence; or at the very least, go haunt something. Instead, he remained restricted within his own tomb. Some kind of energy bound him there. Even when the bronze gates were unlocked and opened for Sarah's interment, he was unable to pass through the portal. His entrapment was frustrating and angered him. Ramsey angered easily anyway. He could feel energy building up within his spirit and it was a bit scary, so he tried to keep it under control.

Ramsey's days passed and ran together, like the colors in the rain. Through his limited vantage point, he watched visitors to the cemetery pay their respects at other gravesites. He took some enjoyment from the occasional shocked faces of visitors who were brave enough to look into his tomb and be surprised by his statue standing in the corner. But even that got old after a few years; he could hardly stand to look at his own effigy anymore.

Ramsey had tried everything he could think of to escape his prison. He thought that if he was indeed in purgatory, maybe he needed to learn some lesson. He examined every moment of his life that he could remember, repenting every selfish or cruel act he had committed. Examining why he had been selfish or cruel, in most cases he found it was because he was angry with himself. He knew he needed to forgive himself, but refused to do so. He figured no one else would absolve him. Why should they? He took houses. He broke up families. In a couple of cases, his actions could have led to individuals committing suicide. Ramsey was pretty sure he deserved to be where he was, but it didn't stop him from wanting out. *If one was content with one's punishment, it wouldn't be punishment now would it?* Those were his thoughts, but he heard them in his mother's voice. He hated that.

Night was worse in Ramsey's crypt. On most nights, the darkness was almost impenetrable. The night of the full moon cast a pale glow across the polished marble as it set in the west, but it also robbed the stone of its color. The long shadows of the bars fell across his statue and seemed to imprison it...mocking how he felt. In the mornings, the sun rose in the east and illuminated the stained glass rendering. Ramsey had not been much for watching television, but he wished he could change the channel on that glass. How many times could St. George slay that dragon anyway? *I get it,* he thought. *You killed a dragon. Was that it? Did you do anything else with your life? The dragon was probably just an allegory anyway.*

"No, I'm pretty sure it was a dragon." Ramsey wasn't sure where the voice came from, but it didn't sound like him. He searched the recesses of his crypt with a mix of excitement and fear. He didn't know if dead people could go insane, but he also didn't know that they couldn't. He felt silly asking, "Who said that?" But he asked anyway. He was almost relieved when he didn't get an answer; but he was also disappointed. *Oh well*, he thought. *Maybe insanity is a gradual process. People just don't go insane overnight. At least, I don't think they do.* Somehow, that thought reassured him.

The nights were boring to say the least, but occasionally a thunderstorm would break the monotony and the silence of the cemetery. One such night changed Ramsey's situation forever. He could tell that a storm was approaching from the west by the sound of the wind and the movement of the trees. A brilliant flash of light was immediately followed by a crack of thunder so strong that it rattled some of the stained glass sections. He had no way of knowing the intense magnitude of the storm or that tornadoes were already touching down nearby. His crypt didn't get weather alerts. If it did, he would have been instructed to find a place of shelter.

The storm raged with an intensity he hadn't experienced since his entombment. Large hailstones began to pelt the bronze doors and leaded glass. When the wind shifted, a series of dull musical notes were produced by the hail hitting the stained glass. There was another crack, but it wasn't followed by the report of thunder. A huge limb, nearly as large as the tree it fell from crashed to the ground, snapping limbs and plowing into the lawn. All of the trees in the cemetery made undulating motions which gave the impression of panic. Ramsey knew nothing could harm him, but he was unnerved by the turmoil anyway. More trees cracked as more limbs fell. Lightning lit up the landscape and thunder crashed. It felt like the end of the world. Ramsey thought his captivity might finally be over. He prepared himself for what was to follow. What followed was silence.

The storm and the wind had abruptly stopped. There was a single cracking noise from somewhere in the cemetery like a gunshot. A weakened limb, which had held on valiantly during the storm, had given up the ghost when the rain and wind stopped. The wail from a civil defense siren in town increased and decreased as it rotated on its mount. It seemed a bit out of place now that the storm had apparently stopped. The ground was littered with hailstones no less than the size of golf balls. Ramsey wished the hail would have damaged his stained glass window, just to change things up from his day to day routine. Still, he was impressed by the craftsmanship and the quality of the piece, even if the hail and wind did loosen a few panes. The window had survived the equivalent of multiple small-scale catapult attacks and was still intact. Saint George would have been proud. Ramsey could hear creaking noises from nearby trees as the wind picked up again. Either there was another weather front approaching or he had been in the eye of the storm. In any event, it began to get rough again.

The strength of the storm had not dissipated. If anything, its intensity had increased. The wind howled through the tree limbs and whistled through the imperceptible gaps in the stained glass. The sound of the civil defense siren was almost lost in the wind. It sounded more like a mournful moan on a Scottish moor than a weather alert. Multiple sounds joined to emphasize the air of chaos. There was a loud clap of thunder, followed by the crack of a huge limb, which was then followed by the shattering of glass and wood as the branch impaled Saint George. If Ramsey had actually been breathing, his breath would have caught in his throat. This was the first real surprise he had received since arriving so many years ago. He didn't hate it.

Saint George had lost his breastplate and his upper torso along with it. His right arm was also missing and Ramsey knew it lay among the shattered glass on the marble floor. Ironically, the dragon was unscathed. More lightning and thunder followed with more shadows and rattles. The rumble of thunder shook the vault for what seemed like an entire minute. Ramsey was exhilarated. He hadn't seen so much activity in a long time. It was like a symphony to him. As a child, he hated thunderstorms; but since his death he had nothing to fear from them. The storm raged on for another three quarters of an hour. Ramsey knew there would be a lot of activity around him for the next few days. The cleanup from the storm would take some time to complete.

The lightning flashes became less intense and the length of time before thunder rolls began to increase. Ramsey knew that the storm was moving on. Small pellets of rain pecked against his window letting him know the storm had had a wonderful time and might come back soon to visit. It departed just as a dull gray dawn began to break in the east. It was a stark contrast to the charged excitement from less than an hour or so before. Large puddles populated the gravel drives throughout the cemetery. A temporary pond covered an entire family plot, leaving only the main family headstone visible above the water. It was going to be a depressing day for most, but not for Ramsey.

He knew that a cemetery cleanup wasn't going to be a priority. There were probably many more pressing emergencies in town. He heard numerous sirens this morning; some were probably for fires, others for medical emergencies. He hoped all went well for the living residents of the community. He could wait for his own excitement to begin. If nothing else, he had learned patience in his time in the afterlife. He suspected it would be a while before anyone would venture into the cemetery. It had a kind of *Land of 10,000 Lakes* quality in which only the most dedicated mourner would brave to visit a lost loved one.

The open space around the branch skewering poor Saint George allowed Ramsey a limited view to the west. Sunsets had always been his favorite and he hoped the window stayed in a state of disrepair long enough for him to catch a few splendid ones. From his new vantage point, he could see only a few grave markers to his right and a row of low shrubs to his left. It wasn't much, but Ramsey was like a child on Christmas morning. He took in every aspect and each nuance of his new perspective; finding that if he concentrated hard enough, he could make out names and dates on some of the stones. *Finally*, he thought. *Fresh reading material!* Ramsey liked to deduce stories from the markers to the east of his crypt. Their dates, ages and proximity to other graves told him stories of the families' triumphs and tragedies. What stories he couldn't deduce from the stones, he made up. No one would know the difference anyway. Now he had new stones and new stories. It wasn't much, but it was all he had.

A fire truck from the town's only fire station sped past the cemetery, even though the road was not one of the more commonly used roads in town. An ambulance could be heard in the distance, its siren blaring as the wail echoed from buildings and hills. The siren suddenly fell silent even though it was nowhere near a hospital, indicating the person being transported was no longer in need of emergency medical attention. That wasn't good. Ramsey felt guilty for his excitement. The cemetery would probably be getting a new resident soon, which wasn't something he should be excited about. His suspicions became more likely when a cleanup crew showed up at the cemetery the very next day. Most of the puddles in the drives had dissipated as the rain water seeped into the ground. There were still a lot of graves underwater though, but there was nothing they could do about that. Ramsey wondered how they dug graves when the ground was saturated with water. The answer was that they didn't. Usually, a service was held, but burial was postponed until the ground was firm enough to dig. The crew was there to make an assessment of the grounds, clear debris and try to make the area presentable.

It took three men to remove the branch from Ramsey's stained glass window. He hadn't realized how big the limb was until they removed it. The lance was as big as a tree in its own right. When they heaved the branch out, it took more of the stained glass with it, including Saint George's other arm, his spear and his head. The dragon again was unharmed. Ramsey began to call the dragon Carson, after a guy he met in a bar one time. The dragon reminded him of Carson for some reason. He wasn't quite sure why. Ramsey had a long talk with the Dragon after that storm. He was glad Carson hadn't been injured and told him so.

The limb took most of the morning to cut up with a chainsaw and haul away. Ramsey watched the whole thing with exquisite relish. The most he had seen from the windows on the east side was the lawn being mowed or leaves being blown. Now there was so much to see that his ethereal senses were nearly overloaded. The few stones he could see before were in the company of rows of stones which extended to a wrought iron fence some distance away. There were small markers and tall obelisks right next to them. Death is no respecter of status nor a respecter of age. The shrubs to Ramsey's left were around a newer section of the cemetery and had a tall pedestal with a white marble statue of a reclining lamb. It was a special area reserved for children and infants. It was an area Ramsey wasn't prepared for or really wanted to see. He turned his attention elsewhere, but was continually drawn back to the activity of the cleanup.

The day passed and the crews left after their work was finished. They didn't return the following day but did the day after that. Ramsey knew why. It was the new resident that the cemetery would now welcome. He wasn't happy with what he knew was coming. They were preparing for a burial in the children's section of the grounds.

Workers busied themselves setting up a heavy tent gazebo for an impending graveside ceremony. There must have been much more space inside the border of shrubs than Ramsey originally thought. A number of chairs were placed beneath the shelter and more behind. It looked as though they were prepared for the entire town to attend. A pedestal with retractable wheels was set in front of a small above ground crypt for one. The dark opening was frightening and sad at the same time. There wasn't anything scary about it really. It was just a reminder of being permanently separated from family and loved ones. No matter what one believed about the afterlife, there was always a lingering doubt that the departed would remain departed.

The clouds parted for a brief period of time. The sun was reflected in a few select puddles throughout the grounds. Some of the grave markers seemed to cast otherworldly glows at its appearance, but Ramsey was sure it was just an illusion of some kind. From the shadows being cast, he estimated it to be around eleven o'clock. The workers didn't seem to have a sense of urgency, so Ramsey suspected the burial would take place later that afternoon. His assumption about the time was substantiated when the workers broke for lunch a half hour later. He felt an odd twist of emotions as he considered the empty chairs draped in black velvet under the sheltering gazebo. Before them was the pedestal which would soon presumably support the casket of a child.

Ramsey turned from his window to compose his thoughts. "That just isn't right," he said. "Maybe there is supposed to be some higher purpose in losing a child, but it still isn't right. There could be other ways to teach a lesson or correct a problem without taking the life of a child. The Universe is twisted."

"You're right; it's a damn shame." Ramsey turned back suddenly to find a face staring through the new opening in the stained glass.

"Can you hear me?" he asked. "See me?"

"Do you think there is anything that can be done about it?" inquired the face. Ramsey was about to answer when another voice answered, "I am sure it could be repaired, but who would authorize it. Everybody connected with this guy is gone. Nobody is going to want to pay for it."

"Isn't the cemetery liable?" questioned the first voice. "...or at least concerned. It won't make a good impression on other visitors."

"Even if they are," remarked the second voice. "I suspect the repair won't be very high on their list of priorities. But you're right Mike; it's a damned shame. Such a fine piece of artwork. We should get back to work. It will be two o'clock soon."

The two men walked off to make their final preparations for what was to come. Ramsey felt like a fool and he had never liked the feeling. He prided himself on being on top of, and if possible, ahead of every state of affairs. He was glad that no one was witness to his humiliation. Ramsey also tended to blow things out of proportion and see conflict where none existed. He wondered how emotions were even possible for his nonexistent body. When he was breathing, he thought emotions were primarily chemical secretions produced by his brain in reaction to outside stimuli. However, he no longer had chemicals, a bloodstream for them to course through, or for that matter, a physical brain. Life had been confusing. Death was even more so.

A long elegant hearse pulled through the gate of the cemetery precisely at two o'clock and stopped across the drive from Ramsey's crypt. The cars following had to park on both sides of the drive to accommodate them all. Everyone seemed hesitant to get out of their cars, even though the driver of the hearse and the funeral director were already at the back of their vehicle. An older man leaned into the limousine which had been leading the funeral procession and was talking quietly to one of the occupants. Everyone else seemed to be waiting for one or more people to disembark from the vehicle before they did likewise.

Finally, a young woman reluctantly stepped out. She was dressed stylishly in black and had a tasteful hat with a black veil. Somehow Ramsey knew that she probably didn't have a lot to do with her attire that day. Someone must have helped her because she was too distraught. The older man who had been talking to her took her arm and she almost collapsed on the spot. He supported her and leaned in to whisper. The woman shook her head noticeably and turned as though she wanted to climb back into the limo. The man embraced her and she cried with her face buried in his chest. Ramsey wished he knew more of the story, but his nonexistent heart was hurting for her as it was. He had so many questions he would have asked if he could.

"That's the mother," said a voice. "Jessica Fielding-Anthony, that's how it was listed in the funeral notice. Such a shame." Ramsey's first instinct was to look up. Then he realized the workers from earlier had discretely positioned themselves near his crypt again. This time, it was to be respectful and unobtrusive.

"Poor little guy," the voice continued. "His name was Charlie. Only six years old."

"I didn't read about it, Mark," whispered a second voice. "What happened?"

"Lightning from that storm a few nights ago struck a tree in their back yard. A treehouse the dad had built for the kid caught fire and the fire spread to the house."

"Horrible! So the little kid was burned up?"

"No," answered Mark. "They got the fire out pretty quickly. He died of smoke inhalation. His lungs weren't very good to begin with is what I heard. He was sickly his entire life. That's how they came to have that crypt."

"The grandfather made the arrangements for it when the kid was about three. He didn't hold out much hope for the boy to survive very long. He was the practical one if you ask me, but I guess his daughter didn't think much of it. She had been holding onto the hope that Charlie would live a long, happy life."

"How the hell do you know all this stuff?" whispered the other worker.

"My wife owns the only beauty salon in town, Michael," explained Mark. "She gets all the intel on everybody and everything. You want to know what I know about you?"

"No," said Michael. "I am perfectly happy in my ignorance."

"Good," replied Mark. "I really didn't have anything anyway."

"So that's the grandfather?" asked Michael. "The one hugging her?"

"Yep," answered Mark. "Nathan Fielding. Used to own the hardware store downtown. He was about to go out of business because of a national chain store moving in near the highway. He sold off his inventory and closed the store. He's not rich but he's pretty well off, I hear."

"Let me guess," said Michael. "Your wife? The beautician?"

"Yes," Mark responded. "…but she prefers the term cosmetologist."

"You mean like an astronaut?"

"I can never tell if you are joking or if you are really that dense," replied Mark.

"Why don't you ask your wife?" There was a long awkward silence and Ramsey didn't know if the two men were smiling, laughing silently, or about to come to blows. He liked the diversion though. It took his mind off the emotive events taking place, at least for a little while. He turned his attention back to the service. The mother, Jessica, was being seated in the first row of chairs under the gazebo.

Her father, Nathan sat down next to her. An empty chair was on her right, presumably for her spouse. Ramsey wondered why he wasn't there or why he didn't ride in the limousine with her.

"Where is the lady's husband?" asked Michael on cue.

"People were taking bets on if he would show up," Mark divulged. "They had a huge fight after they lost the little boy. It's been said that she blames him because he distracted her that night. I think that was a code word for *having sex.* She insists it was his fault that no one got to the boy in time to save his life because he had these *primal urges.*"

"Look at her," said Michael. "How could you not have primal urges for her?"

"Hey! Let's show a little respect here. She just lost a kid!"

"Sorry," offered Michael. Then after a pause, "…but you brought it up."

"Anyway…," Mark continued. "…I had heard they made up. I'm not sure why he isn't here. He isn't the boy's biological father, you know."

"What? I didn't know that," said Michael.

"Yeah, his name is Terry," offered Mark. "He married Jessica while she was still pregnant. The biological father never even knew he had a child on the way. Charlie was the product of a one-night-stand. Nice enough guy though, I guess. She said he was just passing through."

"Oh, crap!" Michael coughed like his throat was dry.

"I know, right? The things that go on," Mark agreed.

"No," exclaimed Michael. "I just realized that MY wife goes to your wife's salon. The crap she must know!"

"You won't be able to look her in the eye when you see her on the street now, will you?"

"I won't have to worry about that," Michael answered. "I'm leaving town! Do you have the number for the witness protection program?" Both men chuckled so loudly that they got several stern looks from the mourners. They ducked behind Ramsey's crypt until the proceedings were over.

Four able-bodied youths had carried the small casket to the pedestal and an arrangement of flowers were placed on top of it. Jessica Fielding-Anthony sat staring at them. It was tough to gage her feelings through the tasteful black veil, but her look seemed to indicate indifference. It was probably shock; perhaps denial; maybe anger. A pastor from a local church presided over the rite and concluded with a prayer. The crowd responded with a somber "amen". Jessica did not participate in the response. She was not feeling "*so be it*". She was enraged inside with, "*What's wrong with you God? Or Universe? Or whatever you are? How could you take my little boy from me? He was my life!*" She was not going to become a party to an antiquated ritual with meaningless chants and empty words. Her entire body was numb except for her head. It felt as if it was on fire and going to explode. Then she saw Terry and a flood of tears gushed forth.

Terry Anthony had been standing back a few yards to keep from intruding on the service. He had really wanted to arrive with the rest of the mourners, but fate had other plans for him. He had gone to the church to talk to God and lost track of the time. Then he had been stopped at a railroad crossing by the slowest train he had ever encountered. Terry loved Charlie and felt his loss as deeply as anyone could. Being blamed for Charlie's death was more devastating than anyone could ever have imagined. Had he known a fire would break out, he would have never left Charlie alone; even if it were to cost him his own life. This was how he felt, but no one would ever consider his feelings. Instead, they thought of him as a step-father with an unwanted child. The community-at-large was certain that if Terry and Jessica had a child of their own, he would cast Charlie aside like a tattered coat. They were wrong, but they would never know it. When people as a whole set their collective minds on something, it takes a miracle to get them to change it. Terry bonded with Charlie the moment he was born. When he found out how serious his illness was, Terry would have given anything to make him well.

Jessica rose on unsteady legs and met Terry as he walked to the graveside. They embraced and his own tears began to flow. He was without words. His heart was lodged in his throat and it was all he could do to breathe. Some of the mourners clasped their hands in front of them and wept for the reunion. Some of the others shook their heads and still stood in judgment of Terry. Those were the ones whose minds would not be changed even if Jesus himself told them that Terry was a good man.

Jessica and Terry both placed a hand on the lid of the small casket. This caused an audible collection of weeping from the crowd. Even some of the judgmental mourners wept openly. Maybe Jesus *did* talk to them. The two workers behind Ramsey's crypt had peeked out to see what the commotion was about. Both of them came down with sudden cases of *sniffles* and *something in my eye*.

The couple stood at the casket for a very long time even after the service was concluded. The other mourners left without expressing their condolences. They left the couple to their private time and thoughts. Even though it was a bit awkward, the attendees got in their cars and quietly left the cemetery until only the hearse and the limo remained. The funeral director waited for what he felt was an appropriate amount of time before going up to the couple and offering his own final condolences. Then he asked them if there was anything else he could do for them. They said no, but shook his hand and thanked him for all he had done already. He quietly said, "Take as much time as you need," and joined the driver in the hearse. The hearse pulled away leaving only Jessica and Terry at the gravesite and Jessica's father, Nathan standing next to the limousine. It felt as though the couples' feet were bound in concrete as they tried to go. They felt like they were abandoning their child; as if they ever could. It was one of the most difficult things they had ever done, but they slowly walked back to the limo.

Terry tried to be strong and keep his eyes focused on the car. Jessica kept looking back, feeling a crush of sadness as she looked at the small casket so isolated in the bleak cemetery. Her legs would have failed her had it not been for Terry's support. When they were seated in the back of the limousine, grief overwhelmed Jessica and she broke down crying. Her husband and father sat helplessly, trying to console her as best they could. Neither really had the heart for consolation because of their own grief and the fronts they were putting up. Jessica bowed her veiled head and Terry realized she had passed out. As a precaution, he took her pulse. He feared perhaps she had expired from the weight of all she was forced to endure. He was relieved to feel a strong pulse and held her hand in both of his as the limousine quietly and respectfully departed from the grounds.

Ramsey gazed at the scene as the limo pulled away. The events had certainly broken the monotony of his day-to-day nonexistence, but not in a way he would have preferred. He didn't remember feeling that much emotion when he was alive. He felt drained; as if he had a personal connection with the family. In a way, he guessed they were neighbors now...almost family. *Death doth make family of us all*, he thought. He apologized to William Shakespeare for butchering the line from Hamlet, but it seemed like an appropriate epitaph of the situation.

With all the mourners gone, the cemetery workers converged on the gravesite like stagehands in a play. Ramsey wasn't sure where some of them had been hiding. Some proceeded to dismantle the gazebo while others collected the chairs. Once that was accomplished, they rolled up the grass carpet and placed it in the back of a mortuary van that Ramsey had not noticed before. Once nearly everything was loaded, there was only one task left to perform. Mark and Michael stood on each side of the small casket and respectfully bowed their heads. After a moment of silence, they lifted the casket by the handles and gently slid it into the above ground vault. Then they secured the marble panel over the opening and made sure it was sealed. A small white placard was held in place by a metal frame. It said *Charles (Charlie) Anthony* and had the year printed below the name. An engraved bronze plaque would be added later. A white wreath was hung on the panel while flowers and stuffed toys were placed at the base of the child's final resting place.

With their duties discharged, the workers left the cemetery and Ramsey was alone once more. The sun peeked through the clouds and the threat of rain seemed to be only that...a threat. The shadows had grown longer and the ambience of the cemetery was that of melancholy reflection. It was not how Ramsey would have chosen to spend his eternal rest. He knew the sun would only be up for a couple of hours before starting its long journey to the next day. He looked out over his domain and imagined the stories he would be able to make of the newly revealed stones. He didn't like the fact that he could still be startled, but he had learned that every new experience was still something to look forward to. That's why he started when he saw the little boy standing next to the newly occupied crypt.

The boy was small and had sandy brown hair. His bright blue eyes looked sad and he seemed so alone. He didn't seem to be wearing clothes, yet he was by no means naked. He seemed to be bathed in an inner light which encompassed his entire body. The boy gazed longingly at the toys at the base of the tomb as if he wanted to play with them, but couldn't.

"Those were mine," the small boy said. He was speaking directly to Ramsey. Ramsey backed away from the stained glass window. He didn't know what to think. *Is this another trick like the one with the workmen?* he thought.

"I didn't get to play with them much," the boy continued. "I was too sick. I'm better now, but I can't feel them."

"Are you Charlie?" asked Ramsey gently.

"How did you know?" demanded Charlie.

"I have people who tell me stuff around here…sort of," replied Ramsey. "I have been here for quite a while. I guess it's where I have to stay."

"Not me," Charlie responded. "I can go wherever I want. I'm just not ready yet."

"What do you mean?" asked Ramsey.

"I need to tell my mommy something," he answered. "…but she's not ready to hear it. She will be soon…but not yet."

"What do you need to tell her, if you don't mind my asking?"

"It's a secret," replied Charlie. "…but I can whisper it." Charlie moved toward Ramsey's crypt. He didn't walk; nor did he float. He sort of phased from one spot to the next until he was inside Ramsey's crypt with him.

"Wow," exclaimed Ramsey. "I wish I could do that."

"You will," offered Charlie. "Someday." The child was so innocent and so sincere that Ramsey could not help but feel a swell of hope which he hadn't felt…ever.

"What makes you think so?" he asked.

"Because everybody has something to do," answered Charlie. "They just don't always know what it is. When they find out, then they can do it."

"I don't know," Ramsey stated. "I have thought of everything and I am still here."

"Well..." said Charlie. "Not everything. You're still here. It is probably something that you don't think is important, but it really is; at least to somebody."

"That is very deep," responded Ramsey. "I guess I will have to think about it some more. Thank you, Charlie. You have given me hope. How did you get so wise? You are like what...six?"

"Six and A HALF," Charlie corrected. He had an air of indignation. "My grandpa used to tell me I have an old soul, whatever that means."

"You certainly do," agreed Ramsey. "You make me wish I had gotten to know my own son."

"Maybe that's your thing," offered Charlie. "You never know."

"You never do," said Ramsey thoughtfully. "Now, what is the secret you need to whisper?"

Charlie looked Ramsey in the eyes and barely moved his spectral lips. "I'm gonna have a sister," he whispered. "Mommy and Daddy are gonna have a baby." He snickered like it was the funniest thing he could think of.

"How do you know?" asked Ramsey.

"Oh, I know things," Charlie stated proudly. "I know LOTS of things."

"I trust you," affirmed Ramsey.

"They need to know that everything will be alright," added Charlie. "…but they aren't ready to know yet. They hurt too much right now…but soon. They will have someone new to care for and things will be better than before. This baby won't be sick all the time."

"You know that wasn't your fault," said Ramsey. "Right?" Ramsey felt the tightness in his nonexistent throat again.

"I know," answered Charlie. "Nobody knows why stuff happens. It feels like we're just stories in a book. The things that happens to us are there to make the story interesting. I'm just not sure who is reading it."

"You are so incredibly deep, Charlie," asserted Ramsey. He was truly impressed.

"I am sure it's not my first time around, if you know what I mean," he responded. "I remember a lot of stuff, but they are things I never did. Some other story I guess; some other lifetime."

"Impressive. So…how long do you think it will be before your mom is ready for the news?"

"Not long," Charlie responded. "If I wait too long, she will find out on her own and that will be bad."

"Why's that," asked Ramsey.

"Because she will feel guilty," Charlie explained. "She will think she is trying to replace me. I can't let that happen."

"How are you going to do that?"

"I will wait a day or so," explained Charlie. "Then I will sneak into her dreams. We'll laugh and hug and play. Then I will tell her about my little sister. It will be so much fun. We will all play together in my mommy's dreams. I will let her know that it's okay to love my baby sister because when she loves her, she will be loving me too."

Ramsey couldn't speak. He couldn't even form coherent thoughts. He felt a great swell of admiration and sadness for this little man and was glad he had become a part of his non-life.

"Do you know what?" Charlie's eyes were innocently wide but all knowing. "You should go to your son. You can talk to him in his dreams. He can be any age in his dreams that he wants. Maybe you can have the little boy you didn't know you always wanted."

"I would have no idea where to begin," Ramsey replied, suddenly finding his voice.

"Maybe that's what you need to think about," suggested Charlie.

"Maybe it is," Ramsey stated. He felt the urge to try to phase through the wall of his crypt. For the first time, he was pretty sure he could do it. He looked down at himself and he glowed with the same inner light he saw coming from Charlie Anthony. Ramsey wasn't going yet though. There might be a great deal more to learn from this young man. He wished he could hug him…and then found that he could.

"Thank you Charlie," exclaimed Ramsey. "Thank you so much!"

-END-

www.ingramcontent.com/pod-product-compliance
Lightning Source LLC
Chambersburg PA
CBHW061544170626
46811CB00001B/75